AMANDA

IN

ALBERTA

THE WRITING ON THE STONE

DARLENE FOSTER

central
avenue
publishing

2014

To Dad

A true cowboy

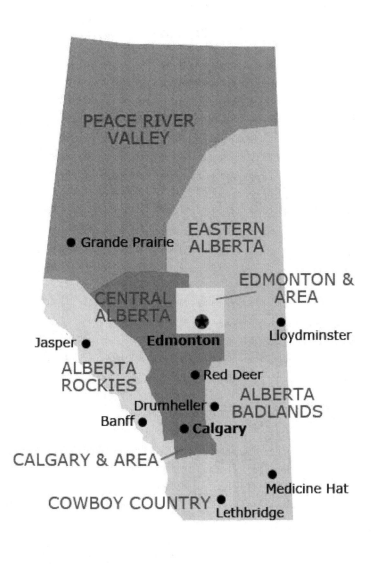

PEACE RIVER VALLEY

EASTERN ALBERTA

● Grande Prairie

EDMONTON & AREA

CENTRAL ALBERTA

Jasper ●

● Edmonton

● Lloydminster

ALBERTA ROCKIES

● Red Deer

ALBERTA BADLANDS

Drumheller ●

Banff ●

● Calgary

CALGARY & AREA

Medicine Hat ●

COWBOY COUNTRY

Lethbridge ●

CHAPTER 1

"Howdy!" A gentleman in a red vest doffed his white cowboy hat. "You look like you might need some help, young lady."

"Where do you meet the people coming from England?" asked Amanda Ross.

"That would be over there at the international arrivals. Are you here to meet a friend?"

"I sure am. Her name is Leah, and she is my BFF coming all the way from England to visit me here in Calgary. I met her in the United Arab Emirates, and then we met in Spain and I visited her in England too. We always have so much fun together. She is way cool."

"I don't think this gentleman needs to know all that, Amanda." Mrs. Ross sent an apologetic look to the airport host. "I finally found a parking spot and noticed Leah's flight has arrived. She should be coming through that door any minute. Amanda, please stand still."

Amanda almost danced, she was so excited. She never had a visitor from overseas before. She carried a stuffed, baby Maine Coon cat; a gift for her friend.

The automatic doors swung open, releasing a flood of travellers.

"There she is! There she is!" Amanda ran up the ramp leaving her mother behind.

Leah wore a VIP badge, dragged a designer wheeler bag and carried a stuffed baby camel. The girls ran towards each other and embraced. They giggled as they exchanged gifts.

"Come and meet my mom." Amanda took Leah's wheeler bag.

"Mom, this is Leah, all the way from England."

"So very pleased to meet you, Mrs. Ross." Leah extended her right hand.

"We've heard so much about you, Leah, and we are very happy you've come for a visit." Amanda's mom shook Leah's hand and popped a white cowboy hat on her blond head. "Call me Evelyn. All Amanda's friends do."

Leah touched the brim of her new hat. "Wowza! A cowboy hat just like Princess Kate got when she came here. Thank you ever so much."

Ω Ω Ω

Amanda and Leah, happy to see each other again, held hands in the back seat and talked nonstop on the drive to the Ross's house.

"So how's your new school, and how's Rupert doing?" asked Amanda.

"My new school is fine and Rupert is doing just great. He's become my best pal and Mum and Dad really like him too. It's like he has always lived with us. He sends you tons of cat cuddles."

"Here we are," said Mrs. Ross as she pulled into a wide driveway.

"My, your house is so large," said Leah as she entered the house.

"It's just an average house here in Calgary," replied Amanda's mom.

"Mom," said Amanda, "houses in England are much smaller."

"Well, I wouldn't know. I'm not the world traveller you are. Why don't you girls visit in the backyard while I get the barbeque ready?"

Amanda led her friend into a spacious backyard surrounded with a lilac hedge.

"We have some fun things planned while you're here; like visiting a dinosaur museum and Head-Smashed-In Buffalo Jump."

"W-what? That sounds dodgy."

"Tomorrow we'll go downtown and watch the Stampede parade."

"I hope you like barbequed hamburgers, Leah." Amanda's mom brought out colourful paper plates and a jug of pink lemonade.

"I love burgers. I seldom get them barbequed. Thanks ever so much, Mrs. Ross—I mean, Evelyn."

Ω Ω Ω

The sun shone brightly as they made their way to downtown Calgary on the crowded C-train the next morning. Thousands of people wearing cowboy outfits lined the streets waiting for the parade. Store fronts were decorated to look like a wild-west town, with bales of hay scattered everywhere. The smell of fried sausages and maple syrup filled the air.

"Let's stop here first for a pancake breakfast."

Amanda's mom pointed to a covered wagon with a long line-up of people, all in jeans, cowboy hats and western shirts. When they got to the front of the line, they noticed a fellow in a huge cowboy hat and a bigger smile flipping pancakes. Another man plunked two pancakes and two sausages on a paper plate. He placed a square of butter on each pancake and poured maple syrup over everything.

"Here you are young ladies. Enjoy," he said as he handed them each a plastic knife and fork rolled up in a paper napkin.

"He put syrup on my sausages," whispered Leah to Amanda.

"Don't worry. It'll be good." They found a shady spot

under a large maple tree where they sat on bales of hay and ate their breakfast.

"Yum, this is good," said Leah as she wiped syrup off her chin.

With full tummies, Amanda's mom led the girls through the swelling crowd to a good viewing spot in front of the high-rise building where she worked. Chairs were set out with a sign that read:

RESERVED FOR D&R ACCOUNTING

"I feel so special," said Leah.

"You should, you are our special guest." Amanda gave her friend's arm a squeeze. "I'm so glad you came for a visit. We'll have so much fun."

Just then a loud BOOM sounded the start of the parade. Amanda and Leah sat spellbound as marching bands in smart uniforms, fancy baton twirlers, cowboys and cowgirls wearing colourful sequinned shirts riding on decorated horses, funny floats and First Nations people wearing traditional feather headdresses passed by.

A clown stopped in front of the girls to hand out candies. He wasn't laughing though. In fact, Amanda thought he looked quite sad. His eyes glanced into the crowd as if searching for someone. He hitched up his baggy pants and an object fell on the ground.

Suddenly, the clown turned around and ran down

the street in his oversized shoes. Children laughed as he almost tripped over his feet.

Amanda shouted after him, "Hey, you dropped something." But he was too far away to hear.

She picked up the stone object, put it in her pocket and continued to watch the parade as a bagpipe band came by.

"I can't believe you have bagpipes over here too. My dad would be impressed. He loves them and used to play in a pipe band," said Leah.

"I love them too," said Amanda. "When they play *Amazing Grace*, I always cry."

"Oh, you definitely would have cried when you heard my dad play. He was awful."

Both girls giggled.

A beaming Stampede Princess wearing a tiara waved at them from her snow white horse.

Ω Ω Ω

Amanda remembered the stone later that night before she went to bed. She took the smooth flat rock out of her jeans pocket and rolled it over in her hand. It was a dark grey colour, about the size of a loonie. She noticed a faint mark on the stone in the shape of a V.

"I wonder what that means," she mumbled.

She placed the rock on her book shelf and crawled into bed beside a jet-lagged Leah already asleep. Happy that her BFF was there with her, she soon fell asleep too.

CHAPTER 2

Amanda's mom served toast at the breakfast bar the following morning. "Are you over your jet-lag, Leah?"

"Oh, yes, Mrs.—I mean Evelyn. I slept well last night."

"It's too bad you missed Amanda's dad. He went into the office early. Hey, how would you like to go to a real ranch with real cowboys?"

"That would be so great. I've only seen ranches on the telly."

"They have way cool horses at the ranch we're going to," said Amanda. She stuffed the rest of the toast in her mouth and jumped off the stool, eager to get going.

Leaving the busy city behind, they drove past golden fields of wheat and through rolling green hills towards the snow capped Rocky Mountains in the distance.

"These are called The Porcupine Hills," said Amanda.

"You do have funny names for places," replied Leah.

"There it is." Amanda pointed to words burnt into a

slice of wood that read:

BAR U RANCH

"Why do you think it is called the Bar U Ranch, Mom?" asked Amanda.

"I believe that's the brand the rancher puts on his cattle to prove they belong to his ranch."

"Do they paint it on?" asked Leah.

"No. They use a hot branding iron to burn it onto the side of the calf. That way it stays on the animal for the rest of its life."

Leah scrunched up her face. "Wouldn't that hurt?"

"Probably. But I don't think it hurts very much," replied Mrs. Ross. "The skin of a cow is leather, so it's tough. Do you remember going to a branding party at your Uncle Jimmy's, Amanda?"

"It was a while ago. I remember I had fun with all my cousins, but I didn't like the burning smell. I felt sorry for the cute baby calves who were crying for their mommies."

Mrs. Ross laughed. "You asked your Uncle if he would please stop hurting the calves. He assured you they would all be back with their mommies soon and would get a special treat for their supper."

They drove through the gate, into the yard, past a large red barn, a log cabin and other red-painted buildings. Once parked, the girls jumped out of the car and were immediately greeted by an excited dog that barked and leapt up to lick their faces.

Leah backed away, but Amanda patted his head and said, "Hi there, Bud. How're you doing?"

"Bart, leave the young ladies alone." A man, his face tanned and wrinkled, grinned and shook Mrs. Ross's hand. "Sorry about that, ma'am, he just loves to get company that's not cowpokes. Welcome to Bar U Ranch. My name's Andy and I'll show you around. This your first time to the ranch?"

"Yes," said Amanda and Leah at the same time.

"She's from England and we wanted to show her a real ranch," said Amanda.

"Well, you've come at the right time. The horses are being exercised right now. Follow me. You don't mind if Bart comes along, do you?"

"Not at all. I love dogs." Amanda gave the grey-blue dog another pat on the head. "What kind of dog is Bart?"

"Bart here is a Blue Heeler. They come from Australia and are great cattle dogs. They need the wide outdoors. Best on a farm or ranch. Not good as house pets."

They followed Andy to a corral where some horses were being led while others wandered around on their own. Two men in one corner of the corral appeared to argue. Amanda glanced in their direction just as one man punched the other in the face. A grey horse near them reared up his front legs. Andy ran over and caught the horse's reins. He spoke softly into his ear until the horse settled down, and then led him back to the large red barn.

Other men broke up the fight. The man who had been hit held his bleeding nose and limped past the girls. He looked directly at Amanda with the saddest eyes she had ever seen. Somehow the eyes looked familiar. She shivered in spite of the hot weather.

Leah continued to watch the magnificent horses walk around the corral. They sauntered very proud and alert, some mostly grey with specks of black while others black with white markings on their heads.

Andy came back from the barn a few minutes later and asked if they would like to go for a wagon ride and see the rest of the ranch.

"Oh, that would be super, wouldn't it Leah?"

The girls climbed up onto an open wagon and sat on bench seats, while Andy held the reins of two large salt and pepper grey horses. "Whoa, Dick. Stand still, Casey. Let everyone get on board before we get a move on." Andy stroked their broad foreheads.

"You sure like your horses. What kind of horses are they?" asked Amanda.

"These are Percheron draft horses. They are the best work horses and extremely intelligent. They are known as the gentle giants of ranching. This ranch is well known for raising Percheron horses over the years."

They toured the ranch at a leisurely pace. Andy pointed out various buildings and told stories about the ranch in the old days. They watched cowhands round up cattle, while Bart barked at the heels of the cows to keep them in line.

"Is that why they are called Blue Heeler dogs; because they are a bluish colour and they bark at the heels of the cows?" asked Amanda.

"You're darned right, young lady. That's exactly why they are called Blue Heelers."

"And why is he called Bart?" asked Leah.

Andy laughed. "When my son was younger, he was a big fan of *The Simpsons*. When we got the puppy, he started calling him Bart and I guess it stuck. He sometimes has an attitude like Bart Simpson, but all in all he's a good dog."

They returned to the cookhouse, where the friendly cook offered them milk and cookies fresh out of the oven.

"Why were those men fighting?" Amanda asked Andy as she sipped the cold milk.

"Oh, it was nothing. The hot weather lately tends to get the cowpokes a bit testy is all," said Andy. "Upstairs is the bunkhouse where the ranch hands slept after a hard day on the trail. Take your time and look around."

After finishing the refreshments, the girls and Amanda's mother checked out the rest of the cookhouse. One room contained two large round tables, fitted with lazy-susans in the middle.

"I guess this is where they ate," commented Leah.

Upstairs they found rows of single beds. Some beds were neatly made with personal items stowed away underneath or stacked on shelves. Other beds were in a tangle and the person's items in disarray.

Amanda walked over to a bed covered with a red and grey striped wool blanket. On the bed was an open fiddle case, a cribbage board and a newspaper open to a page with an advertisement for a western jamboree. The bedside table consisted of a wooden apple crate on its side, the bottom lined with books. On top sat a picture of a pretty young girl with braids and a cowboy hat. Beside the picture rested a couple of smooth rocks. Amanda, tempted to pick them up and examine them, was startled by a man rushing up the stairs. She noticed he had bright red hair.

"Sorry to disturb you folks," said the cowboy out of breath. "I forgot something here earlier."

"We should be going anyway." Amanda's mom steered the girls down the stairs.

As they were about to leave the cookhouse, Amanda noticed some rocks behind glass doors in a cupboard.

"Look at all these cool rocks. Were did you get them?"

"People who lived and worked here have been collecting them over the years. If you look closely, many are fossils. It's hard to imagine, but this entire area used to be a sea bed. You'll notice seashells embedded in some of the rocks," explained Andy.

Amanda noticed a dark grey rock with interesting marks on it. "What do those marks mean?"

"I don't know. They may be pre-historic. Perhaps a form of written language."

Amanda thought the marks looked similar to the one on the stone the clown dropped.

Chapter 3

Leah opened the fridge door to get the milk for breakfast.

"Good morning," said an unfamiliar voice.

Leah leapt back and almost dropped the milk.

"You must be Leah," said a slim man in a T-shirt and jeans. "I'm Don, Amanda's dad. Sorry if I startled you." He took the milk from Leah's shaky hand and placed it on the table. "Sorry I wasn't here to meet you yesterday. Busy at the office. But, I have today off. I hope you've been having a nice time so far." His smile was warm and welcoming.

"Oh yes. It has been good. I loved the Stampede parade and the visit to the ranch. This place is amazing. I feel like I'm on American telly."

"I see you've finally met my dad." Amanda appeared, straight from the shower, her hair almost dripping. "I'll have some of that cereal too."

Amanda's mom walked in wearing a blue satin cowboy shirt with horseshoes embroidered on the collar and cuffs. "Great. Everyone's up. Today we're all going to the Calgary Stampede. How long until you're ready, girls?"

Amanda jumped off the breakfast stool. "I just need to dry my hair and get dressed."

Leah watched Amanda as she put on her newest pair of jeans and a wide leather belt with a horseshoe belt buckle. A red and white checked shirt that matched her red straw cowboy hat completed the outfit.

"You look fab. But what am I going to wear? I don't have any cowboy clothes."

Amanda threw Leah a Riley & McCormick bag.

"Try this."

Leah pulled out a white western shirt with pearl snaps and a red yoke, collar and cuffs. The front was embroidered with colourful flowers.

"Wowza! This is terrific. It will go so well with my jeans and the white cowboy hat your mom gave me."

Two young cowgirls emerged from the bedroom. Amanda's mom took a picture.

Ω Ω Ω

The sign above the entrance to the Stampede grounds read:

Welcome to the Greatest Outdoor Show on Earth

The grounds teemed with people. The smells of buttered popcorn, foot-long hot dogs and candied apples

16

mixed with the scents of dust and livestock.

"This is like a huge carnival," exclaimed Leah.

"What ride should we go on first?" asked Amanda.

"Let's go on the Ferris wheel," suggested Amanda's mom.

"Kind of like a small London Eye," said Leah as they got buckled in.

They overlooked barns and corrals, concession stands, games with stuffed animals for prizes, other rides and an Indian village as they got to the top.

"What's that building?" Leah pointed. "It looks sort of like a horse's saddle?"

"That's the Saddledome," replied Amanda. "It's where they play hockey and have concerts; like Justin Bieber and Lady Gaga."

"Have you been to any of the concerts?"

"No, Mom says I'm too young."

They went on a few more rides. Amanda's dad won a stuffed cow at a shooting gallery which he gave to Leah. They munched on corn dogs and candy floss.

"Now it's time for the rodeo." Mr. Ross led them to their seats on the grandstand. They watched cowboys get thrown off raging bulls and rescued by clowns. Cowgirls rode around barrels with precision, waving their hats to the crowd when they finished. Bronco riders in leather chaps, and spurs on their cowboy boots waited their turn at riding a wild stallion.

"That looks dangerous," commented Leah.

"It is. The cowboy has to stay on the bucking bronco for at least eight seconds. The one who stays on the longest wins and gets paid a lot of money. They figure it's worth it," explained Amanda's dad.

Just then, the chute opened and a fierce horse emerged, trying hard to buck the rider off; which he did successfully before the eight seconds was up. The cowboy face-planted into the dirt. A clown immediately jumped off the fence, distracted the horse by holding up a pair of red flannel underwear and pretended to be a bull fighter. The crowd roared with laughter. The bowlegged cowboy picked up his ten gallon hat, slapped it against his leg and limped away. The clown took hold of the reins, whispered something into the horse's ear and led him in the opposite direction.

Amanda looked over at the fence where the clowns sat. One clown dug in his baggy pants pocket as if looking for something. She wasn't sure but he looked a bit like the clown at the parade. She reminded herself that all clowns look alike in their make up and costumes.

As the rodeo came to an end, Amanda's mom asked, "Did you girls enjoy that?"

"Yes, thank you very much," said Leah.

"It was OK, but I didn't like that the people and the animals could get hurt," said Amanda.

"I liked how the clowns rescued the cowboys and made the crowd laugh," said Leah.

"The clowns have the hardest job of all," replied Amanda's dad. "Many of them are actually bullfighters, hired to distract the animal and expose themselves to great danger in order to protect the cowboy. Others are hired to entertain the crowd. Under those bright, loose fitting costumes, they wear protective gear. They work in teams and have to be in excellent shape because what they do is dangerous."

Amanda wanted to visit the Indian Village, so they went around the back of the rodeo grounds and past the barns. Angry voices could be heard near one of the barns. As they got closer, they saw two rodeo clowns arguing. The taller fellow pulled on the shorter clown's suspenders.

"Where is it? I know you have it. I want it now."

"I don't have it, I tell you. I must've lost it."

"Well, I don't believe ya, you lying son..."

"Excuse me," interjected Mr. Ross. "There are children here."

Both clowns turned around, surprised.

"Sorry sir, madam." The taller clown tipped his battered cowboy hat, revealing red hair. "We were just practicing a routine we plan to use tomorrow. Enjoy yourselves now, folks."

They both turned and walked into the barn, but not before Amanda made eye contact with the short clown. She recognized his sad eyes.

CHAPTER 4

Amanda's parents walked the girls over to the entrance to the Indian Village.

"Your father and I are going for a coffee," said Amanda's mom. "We'll meet you back here in an hour." The girls smiled at each other, thankful for a bit of time alone together and turned towards the entrance.

"*Oki*. Welcome to our Indian Village." A young man wearing a feather headdress greeted them with a welcoming smile. "My name is Dan Crow Feather and I will be pleased to show you around our village."

Twenty-six colourful tipis sat arranged in a circle just as they would have been hundreds of years ago.

"Can we see inside a tipi?" asked Amanda.

"Of course, follow me." Dan led them to a white tent trimmed in red, with a large black buffalo painted on the side. Small animals that looked like dancing dogs decorated the bottom. He opened a flap and said, "Grandmother, we have visitors."

It took a couple of minutes for the girls to adjust to the dim smoky light. Bedrolls lined the circle and multi-coloured woven rugs covered most of the floor. In the centre an older woman sat near a small fire. She held a stick over the flame. A colourful shawl covered her shoulders and a long salt and pepper braid trailed down her back. She looked up and smiled as the girls entered.

"Welcome. Would you like some bannock? I just made some fresh."

She took a round piece of what looked like a biscuit off the end of the stick, broke it in two and put it on a tin plate. She handed the plate to Amanda and Leah. They each politely took a piece.

Amanda bit into hers and asked, "What is bannock?"

"It's Indian bread, made with flour, baking powder and water, and fried in fat or cooked on a stick over an open flame. It has long been a staple of the Indian diet," explained Dan.

"It's very good, thank you," said Leah.

"I see you come from England," said the grandmother.

"Yes, I am here visiting my friend, Amanda."

"When I was a young woman, I met your Queen Elizabeth. She came to the Calgary Stampede and visited the Indian Village. She was very nice and said it was her favourite thing she saw."

"That is awesome!" exclaimed Amanda.

"Grandmother loves to tell everyone about meeting

the Queen. She used to be a Jingle Dress Dancer when she was a girl your age."

"Can you tell us more about the tipis and what it's like to sleep in one?" asked Amanda.

"Well, we don't sleep in tipis anymore, but use them for occasions like this when we re-enact life as it once was. Surprisingly, they are quite comfortable. They are very durable, providing warmth in the cold prairie winters and coolness in the hot summers. They also kept the rain out during our heavy downpours. They were originally made of animal skins but are now made of canvas. Tipis are designed to be taken down and packed away quickly when the tribe had to move. This happened often for the Plains Indians as they searched for food."

They finished eating the bannock and said goodbye to the grandmother. Once back outside, Amanda asked Dan, "What about the paintings on the tipis?"

"Not all tipis are painted. They can be decorated with images of celestial bodies like the brown tipi with orange circles representing the sun over there." Dan pointed. "Often they represent personal experiences such as a war or animals that a family member hunted successfully like deer, buffalo or bears."

Amanda looked closely at the paintings on Dan's family tipi. The huge buffalo took up one side. The smaller animals she thought were dogs looked more like wolves close up. Around the wolves were small marks similar to the V on the stone in her bedroom.

Dan looked at his watch, "If we hurry, we can catch the Jingle Dress Dance at the Stampede Pow-Wow Stage."

"What's a Jingle Dress Dance and what's a Pow-Wow?" asked a puzzled Leah.

"A Pow-Wow is a dance competition. You'll soon see," explained Dan.

They approached a grandstand on which stood young girls wearing bright red, green, yellow, and blue dresses. Each dress was decorated with rows of shiny cones on the sleeves, tops and along the bottoms of the skirts. The dancers wore beaded leather moccasins on their feet, eagle plumes in their hair and carried feather fans. When drummers started to beat the drums; each girl placed a hand on one hip and began dancing in a pattern, feet close to the ground. As they danced around, the shiny cones made a cheerful jingling sound.

"Wow! This is incredible. If only I could dance like that," said Amanda. "Those girls are only about eight years old and they are so good."

"I love their colourful outfits," said Leah.

"Some of these girls learn the Jingle Dress Dance when they are only three or four years old. They go all over North America entering Pow-Wow competitions.

My sister is the girl in the green dress." Dan pointed her out.

"What are the little bells made of?" asked Leah.

"The jingles are usually made of lids from chewing tobacco tins rolled into cones." Dan laughed. "At least something good comes out of tobacco."

Everyone clapped and cheered when the dance was over. Dan's sister came over to say hello with a huge grin.

"Sharon, I would like you to meet our guests, Amanda and Leah. Leah has come all the way from England."

"I absolutely loved your performance. I can't wait to tell my mates back home," exclaimed Leah.

"Would you like a picture with Sharon?"

"Would we ever!" Amanda stood on one side of the Jingle Dress Dancer and Leah stood on the other. Dan snapped a picture with Leah's camera.

"Thanks for showing us around, Dan. It was so great to meet you, Sharon. We must get back to the entrance to meet my parents."

"Glad you stopped by. Enjoy the rest of your holiday, Leah." Dan waved goodbye.

The girls got to the gate a few minutes before Amanda's mom and dad showed up. As they waited, two men in cowboy hats walked by involved in a serious conversation.

"Didn't that look like Andy from the ranch and the

guy that was in the fight?" asked Amanda.

"Everyone here looks the same to me in cowboy hats and jeans," replied Leah. "Now, where can I buy some of those chill cowboy boots everyone is wearing?"

CHAPTER 5

"Mom, Leah wants to buy some cowboy boots. Can we take her shopping today?" asked Amanda the next morning.

"Sure, that would be fun. We can stop at the *Cowboy Boot Warehouse* on MacLeod Trail and then head out to your uncle's farm. They're expecting us for lunch."

Amanda gave Leah's arm a squeeze. "You'll get to meet my farm cousins."

"How many do you have?"

"Ten." Amanda held up all her fingers.

"All in the same family?" Leah's eyes grew larger.

"Oh yes. Uncle Jimmy and Aunt Marjorie had one kid a year, except one year they had a set of twins. Uncle Jimmy said instead of hiring extra help on the farm, he produced his own." Amanda giggled. "Uncle Jimmy is a funny guy. You'll see."

"I have only two cousins and I never see them."

"Well, you can share some of mine then." Amanda grabbed Leah's hand as they headed towards the SUV.

Ω Ω Ω

The warm smell of leather greeted the girls when they entered the *Cowboy Boot Warehouse*.

Leah looked around in amazement. "I...I wouldn't know where to start."

Shelves full of boots of all colours and styles lined the walls and filled the centre of the store. Boots even hung from the ceiling.

"Let's start with your size." Amanda's mom led them to the correct area of the store. "You girls start trying on boots while I look at some in my size."

Amanda had fun picking out boots for Leah to try on. Soon a mound of boots surrounded them. They giggled as they surveyed the assortment. Just then a young man appeared around a corner.

"May I help you?" He looked surprised. "Oh—hello again."

"Hi Dan!" said both girls at once when they recognized the boy from the Indian Village.

"Do you work here?" asked Amanda.

"Yes, this is my part-time job. I'm saving up to go to university when I graduate from grade twelve next year."

He looked at the boots scattered about. "Are you planning to buy all of these?"

Leah blushed. "I just can't decide. They're all so rad."

Dan picked up a pink, pointy-toed boot stitched with swirls of flowers and a white top embroidered with pink flowers. "Try these on, Leah."

Leah pulled them on over her skinny jeans.

"Walk over to the mirror and have a look."

Leah viewed herself in the long mirror.

"You sure rock those boots, Leah," exclaimed Amanda.

"How do they feel? It's important that they're comfortable," said Dan.

"They feel like they were made just for me." Leah beamed. "I don't want to take them off. My mates in England are going to be ever so jealous."

"Great! What about you, Amanda?" He chose a red pair embroidered with small white flowers with stars as centres. "I think these would suit you just fine."

"Have you found anything you like?" Mrs. Ross arrived holding a dark brown pair of boots decorated with blue birds and red roses.

"Dan helped us pick out the best in the store."

"You are a fine salesperson, Dan. Where do I pay for all of these?"

"He sure is a good salesperson." A man in a black cowboy hat slapped Dan on the back.

Dan jumped. "Uncle Ed, stop doing that. You scared me out of my wits." He grinned at the man. "I'd like to introduce you to my new friends, Amanda and her friend Leah who is visiting from England. This, I assume, is your mother, Amanda?"

"Oh, yes. Sorry. Mom this is Dan Crow Feather. Dan this is my mom."

"Nice to meet you, Amanda's Mom. You can take your purchases over to the counter in the middle. Make sure you mention that Dan assisted you."

Mrs. Ross left the girls chatting as she paid for the boots.

Amanda noticed a bruise on Uncle Ed's face. "Weren't you at the Bar U Ranch the other day when we visited?"

"Ya, I was. Sorry you had to see the fight." Ed looked down at his feet.

"Uncle Ed works at the ranch when he isn't being an artist or a rodeo clown."

"Dan! Now you've blown my cover." Ed punched his nephew on the shoulder.

"Sweet! I've never met a rodeo clown before. Isn't it scary being face-to-face with those ferocious horses?" asked Amanda.

"Naw. I know they won't hurt me. I just whisper sweet nothings in their ears and they calm right down."

"What kind of art do you do?" asked Leah.

"Now that's my real job. The one I love. I do paintings and carvings. Too bad I don't make enough money at it."

"Uncle Ed does some wonderful work. He has a small studio in Bragg Creek. You should visit it if you go there," Dan added.

Amanda's mom arrived carrying three bags. "All set, girls. Let's get going." She nodded her head, "Nice to meet you, Dan...Ed."

As they turned to leave the store, Amanda heard Dan say to his uncle, "Have you found it yet?"

Ed replied, "No, but I'm sure that ranch hand took it. I just don't know how to get it back."

On the drive out of town Amanda pondered what she heard and wondered if she should tell someone about the rock with the carving on it. 'Am I wrong in keeping it? Is it valuable? Is that even what they were talking about?'

Her thoughts were interrupted when they turned into a farmyard. Yelping dogs greeted them along with a number of shouting children. Amanda jumped out of the vehicle, petted the dogs and hugged the small children. Leah, looking uneasy, stayed inside.

A young girl approached the SUV and said, "You must be Leah. I'm Sarah, Amanda's cousin. I've heard all about you. Welcome to our farm." She reached out her hand to help Leah out of the jeep. "Don't worry about the dogs and kids, they're crazy but harmless."

Sarah led everyone into the farmhouse filled with the smell of cabbage rolls, roasted ham and fresh baked bread.

Amanda introduced Leah to her Aunt Marjorie who

was busy in the kitchen.

"Please sit down. Lunch is ready. Great Aunt Mary is here already."

An elderly woman in a plaid shirt looked up from under her round glasses. A thick braid of white hair circled her head. Her weather worn face broke into a wide grin when she saw the visitors.

Amanda gave the woman a big hug and introduced her to Leah. "Aunt Mary is a palaeontologist. She knows all about fossils and dinosaurs and stuff. She used to work at the dinosaur museum."

Just then a man in dungarees and a straw hat entered the room.

"What's this? I don't remember inviting all of you people for lunch. I have enough kids to feed as it is. And who is this city slicker?" He picked up Amanda and swung her around.

"Uncle Jimmy, you are such a kidder."

"Eat up folks. Marjorie's been cooking all morning and we don't want any leftovers. If you clean your plates, there will be horse rides after lunch."

The children squealed with delight as they dug into their food. Everyone talked at once. Leah looked confused by the commotion.

Aunt Mary leaned over and asked, "Do you come from a large family, Leah?"

"No," she answered. "There is just me and my mom

and dad. And Dad is often away working."

"Then this hullabaloo must be quite overwhelming for you. We'll do something quieter after we eat."

Amanda was pleased to see that Aunt Mary and Leah were chatting. She thought she might ask Aunt Mary about the stone later.

CHAPTER 6

Four horses waited by the barn, saddled up and ready to go. Uncle Jimmy helped Amanda onto a chestnut-brown he called Ginger. He then gave Leah a hand to mount a black and white.

"Tonto is a dependable horse who will look after you," he assured Leah.

Sarah and Aunt Mary mounted black stallions.

Amanda looked over at Leah with a wide grin. "Do you think you'll like riding horses better than camels?"

"Oh, yes. I like horses. I took riding lessons in England the summer we lived in York."

"You sure have lived in lots of different places."

"My dad's job takes him to many locations. Mum and I go with him when we can."

Sarah pulled up alongside. "That sounds exciting. I never get to go anywhere."

"You should come with Amanda the next time she visits me," replied Leah.

"Mom always needs me to help out on the farm. I probably wouldn't be able to get away." Sarah looked down at her hands.

"Follow me, girls." Aunt Mary led them through the farm gate and down a hill toward a clump of trees. "If we follow this path, we'll get to Sheep River Falls. It's a good ride and very pretty when we get there." She looked over her shoulder. "Are you OK back there?"

"We're fine, Aunt Mary," replied Amanda.

The older woman skilfully guided them through the trees and over more rolling green hills. "We call these the foothills," she explained.

In the distance, rugged, snow-capped mountains poked toward the sky.

"Are those the Rocky Mountains?" asked Leah.

"Those are the famous Rocky Mountains," replied Aunt Mary. "I've lived in these parts all my life, and I'm still astounded by them."

"They look awesome, and so very huge." Leah rode ahead with Sarah.

"Aunt Mary," asked Amanda, "I know you do some work at the dinosaur museum, and you know a lot about history and stuff. What do you know about stones with writing on them?"

"Actually, I'm in the midst of doing some research on prehistoric stones with marks on them which could be very important. Why do you ask, dear?"

"Well, I found a flat, smooth stone. It has a mark on it that looks like it could mean something, but I don't know if it's important or not."

"Let me have a look at it sometime and I'll let you know. Where did you find it?"

Before Amanda could answer, three riders came up behind them. Amanda swung around, startled. 'Where did they come from?' she thought.

"Well, howdy!" The man leading the group grinned when he saw Amanda and Leah. "Fancy seeing you fillies here on the trail."

"Hi, Andy!" exclaimed Amanda. "We're going on a trail ride with my Aunt Mary."

"Howdy, Mrs. Johnson. How you doing these days?" Andy tipped his hat. "How's your research coming along?"

"Just fine, Mr. Rowlands. Just fine." Aunt Mary answered with a furrowed brow. "What brings you out here?"

"Getting ready for a cattle drive and rounding up a few strays."

Rustling came from a clump of bushes and a yelping dog emerged.

"What is it, Bart? Did you get stung by a bee?" Andy jumped off his horse, knelt down and felt around the shivering dog. "Ah, here it is." Andy pulled something hard and prickly from behind the dog's back leg. "It's a burr. They can stick on a dog and drive him crazy if he can't get it off. This one was in an awkward place." He patted the dog's head and scratched his chin. "There ya go, fella. You'll be OK. Now, go find those strays."

Andy stood up and walked over to Amanda. He stroked Ginger's back while he said under his breath, "I heard you found an interesting stone. You know I collect stones. You might want to add it to my collection." Then louder he said, "Have a good ride, girls, ma'am. The weather is perfect for it. Nice to see you all." He climbed back on his horse and rode off with the other two men, leaving a trail of dust.

Amanda felt uneasy as they continued on their way. 'How did Andy know I have the stone? Did he hear me mention it to Aunt Mary? What did he mean by me adding it to his collection and why was Aunt Mary not very friendly to him'?

The bright sun shone on the riders as they wound their way further up into the hills and through majestic pine trees. Soon they came to a river.

"How will we cross?" asked Amanda.

"Don't worry. These horses are used to crossing water. Sheep River is not very wide and it's shallow here. They can walk across. But if they had to, they could swim," explained Aunt Mary as she coaxed her mount into the water.

Sarah followed her. Amanda looked over at Leah who had a worried look on her face.

"We'll be all right. Aunt Mary knows what she's doing. Our feet won't even get wet."

She let Leah go ahead of her. Tonto walked into the crystal clear water and immediately bent down to have drink.

Leah gasped. "Oh no! I'm...I'm going to fall off." She gripped the reins with both hands.

Aunt Mary and Sarah shouted from the other bank, "Come on, Tonto. Stop fooling around."

The horse raised his head, shook it from side to side spraying Leah with water, and continued on as if nothing had happened. Amanda laughed.

"That was majorly unfunny. I'd appreciate it if you didn't laugh."

"Don't English horses get thirsty?" asked Amanda.

"Perhaps, but they wait until I'm off before they have a drink."

Rumbling water could be heard in the distance. A few minutes later they rounded a bend and found themselves in front of water cascading over slabs of rock.

"Wowza!" exclaimed Leah. "This is some sweet waterfall. Did you say it was called Sheep River Falls?"

"It's called Sheep River Falls because there are many big horn sheep in the area," said Aunt Mary.

"Will we see some?" asked Amanda.

"Probably not. When it gets warm like this, they tend to go up higher in the mountains to keep cool. Let's let the horses have a rest and a drink while we stretch our legs." Aunt Mary pulled out some canteens of water from her saddlebag. "I think we all need a drink too."

The water tasted cold and fresh.

"Yum. That's so good. Why does water always taste better from a canteen?" asked Amanda.

BOOM!

Amanda jumped, spilling water down the front of her shirt. A thorny red flash shot across the distant mountains.

Aunt Mary glanced up at the dark cloud that suddenly appeared, blotting out the sun. "We'd better head back. Looks like we might be in for a sudden thunder shower."

Amanda shivered.

Chapter 7

Prepared for everything, Aunt Mary pulled out rain ponchos for everyone from her saddlebags.

Amanda giggled when she saw Leah in her bright yellow poncho with a pointy hood. "You look like Big Bird."

"Well then, you look like a mini Big Bird," Leah retorted.

"Sarah, you take the lead," said Aunt Mary. "I'll follow behind to make sure everyone is all right."

Another loud crack came from the mountains, followed by streaks of lightning across the darkened sky.

"Is it possible that we could be struck by lightning?" asked Leah, glancing behind her.

"Not likely," answered Aunt Mary. "The lightning is not very close."

The rain came down in torrents. Amanda had trouble seeing through the huge droplets on her glasses. The raindrops hurt when they hit her arms and legs. Water ran down into her runners. "Yuck! I hate this rain. Where did it come from so suddenly?"

"If you don't like the weather in Alberta, just wait a few minutes and it will change," said Sarah.

"Ouch. These raindrops are really starting to hurt."

"That's because it's no longer rain, it's hail," replied Aunt Mary.

Amanda looked ahead. Frozen balls of ice, the size of marbles, bounced off the ground. Soon the trail turned white. It looked like snow—in July.

"Let's head over there, under the trees for shelter," suggested Aunt Mary.

"Are you OK, Leah?" asked Amanda once they were away from the hail. "It won't last long. It never does."

"I've never seen hail like this before. The horses don't seem to be bothered though." Leah patted Tonto.

As quickly as it started, the hail ended and turned to rain, melting the white balls and leaving no evidence.

When they arrived at the river, a much different scene appeared before them than when they crossed it earlier. The water had risen with the downpour and it flowed much faster. Small whirlpools appeared in the centre.

"I don't think we should cross," said a worried Amanda. "I-I'm not a very good swimmer."

"You'll be all right. Your horse can swim. Just hang on. Look, Sarah is halfway across already," assured her aunt.

Amanda coaxed the horse into the raging river. The

cold water covered her already wet runners and the bottom of her jeans. She squeezed her eyes shut and whispered, "Get us across safely, Ginger."

Soon she was on the other side with her cousin. She dismounted and turned to watch Leah cross on Tonto. Halfway across, Leah's saddle tilted to one side. Leah tried to straighten up but it kept slipping over. A whirlpool circled Tonto's legs, spooking him. He lifted his front legs and Leah went crashing into the angry water.

Amanda stared into the swirling water searching for her friend. "Leah!" she screamed when she couldn't see her.

Then she saw Leah's head bob and started to run toward the river.

"Stay where you are," ordered her aunt.

Amanda stood on the shore feeling helpless.

Aunt Mary charged into the water, jumped off her horse and swam toward Leah. She put her arms around the young girl and swam with her to the shore.

"Is she all right?" Amanda ran to help drag her soggy friend to the river bank.

Leah coughed and sputtered. "I'm...I'm OK. Thanks to your aunt." She shook her drenched head. "She sure is a strong swimmer, for an eighty year old."

"She swims at the pool three times a week," explained Amanda. She looked over at the riverbank. "Is everything OK? Aunt Mary?"

The older woman's face turned white as she clutched her chest. She gasped for air and couldn't seem to get any words out. She just shook her head. Then she fell forwards.

"I think she's having a heart attack! Sarah and Leah, go for help. I'll stay with her."

"No," said Leah. "I'll stay with her while you two get help. She just saved my life. I will not let anything happen to her."

Sarah brought the horse blanket from Aunt Mary's horse and tucked it around her shivering body. "Let's go. I know the way."

"We'll be back as soon as possible, Leah," assured Amanda. "Everything will be all right." She gave her friend a weak smile.

Sarah and Amanda hadn't ridden far when they heard barking. They rounded a grove of poplar trees and a dog ran up to them with his tail wagging.

"Bart!" Amanda slowed her horse. "Is Andy close by? Can you lead us to him?"

The dog barked, ran around in a couple of circles and darted back through the trees.

"Let's follow him," said Amanda.

"Are you sure? Maybe we should go straight back to my house." Sarah frowned.

"This could be faster." Amanda headed for the trees. She soon heard a man's voice on the other side.

"What is it, boy?"

Coming through the trees, they saw Andy kneeling down and patting Bart's head. He glanced up and smiled. "What have we here? Where is the rest of your party?" Andy stood up abruptly. "By the look on your faces, I sense something's gone wrong."

"It's Aunt Mary. She pulled Leah out of the river, and now I think she's having a heart attack or something. Leah's with her and we need to get her to a doctor."

Andy whipped out his cell phone like a gunslinger pulling out his weapon at a gunfight. He called 911 for an ambulance and then Sarah's dad.

"We need to get her to the road. Good thing we have the chuck wagon with us. We had planned an overnighter. Good job, Bart. That dog can always sense trouble."

They were soon back at the river. Aunt Mary looked awful, but managed a faint smile when Andy said, "Don't you worry, Mrs. Johnson. We have everything under control, thanks to these quick thinking young ladies here."

Andy and a ranch hand loaded the older woman into the chuck wagon and took her and the girls to a nearby road where an ambulance waited. Uncle Jimmy and Amanda's mom arrived a few minutes later.

"Leah, Amanda, are you all right?" Mrs. Ross looked frantic. "I should have never let you go on the trail ride.

Leah, you're shivering. We need to get you in the car right now. Jimmy can bring the horses home."

Amanda held Leah's hand in the car. "I'm so glad you're OK. You sure had me worried for a minute there. I hope this hasn't ruined your holiday."

"Oh no, not at all. It has turned into a great adventure." Leah's icy cold hand squeezed Amanda's hand. "I'm sure glad you came back with help as quickly as you did."

"You can thank Bart. That dog came to our rescue."

CHAPTER 8

After mugs of hot chocolate, showers and a good night's sleep, the girls felt much better the following morning.

"How's Aunt Mary?" asked Amanda as she slid onto a breakfast bar stool.

"I called the hospital and she's doing just fine. It was a mild heart attack, thank heaven. She's a tough old bird, that one." Amanda's mom divided banana slices on top of two bowls of cereal.

"Can we go and visit her?"

Mrs. Ross placed a bowl in front of each girl. "Of course, dear. I thought we'd stop in at the Foothills Hospital on our way to Bragg Creek."

Amanda burst into a huge smile. "Bragg Creek! Leah, you will love it there. Maybe we can visit Dan's uncle's studio. I'd love to see his art."

"Sounds good," said Leah. "Just as long as we don't have to cross a river...on a horse...in a storm."

"I'm so sorry about that, Leah. Uncle Jimmy feels terrible. He was sure he had tightened the cinch of that saddle. It was so awful watching you as the saddle slipped sideways," said Amanda.

"I'd have been all right if Tonto hadn't spooked."

"That's the other thing Jimmy couldn't understand. Tonto should be used to fast running rivers." Amanda's mom shook her head then said, "Eat up so we can get this show on the road."

Ω Ω Ω

Aunt Mary's face lit up when all three walked into the room with a large bouquet of flowers. "Evelyn, you shouldn't have. Thanks so much. And thanks for bringing these two heroines to see me."

She received hugs from everyone.

"I'm so sorry for endangering your lives. I never foresaw that terrible rain and hailstorm. To think my dear departed husband was a meteorologist. May he rest in peace. I just don't understand what got into that horse, Tonto. It was like he had a burr under his saddle."

"It sure was good that we found Andy nearby," said Amanda.

"Yes, he can be a good sort...sometimes." Aunt Mary sighed.

"Come, girls." Mrs. Ross motioned. "We'd better let Aunt Mary rest. We're off to Bragg Creek but I need to drop off some papers to a client in Cochrane first. Maybe we can stop for ice cream while we're there."

Leah's eyes almost popped out of her head when she saw the wall of flavours at *MacKay's Ice Cream*. It didn't take her long to choose a scoop of caramel apple pie ice cream in a vanilla waffle cone.

"Come on, Amanda, make up your mind. We don't have all day." Mrs. Ross tapped her on the shoulder. "You can never make up your mind when we come here."

Amanda finally decided on a scoop of cherry custard ice cream in a regular cone.

"This has got to be the best—ever!" said Leah as she licked the ice cream running down the side of the cone.

Ω Ω Ω

Once in Bragg Creek, the girls walked down the boardwalk arm in arm, looking in the many shop windows.

"My mum would just love this place," said Leah.

"Perhaps you can buy her something from here to take back home," suggested Mrs. Ross as they passed another gift shop.

Amanda spotted a bookstore called *The Best Wordhouse in the West* when Leah shouted, "Hey, do you think this could be the shop belonging to Dan's uncle?" They stood in front of a window displaying First Nations' art. "Let's check it out."

Inside they found an assortment of unique items such as beaded bags and moccasins, hand carved animals and bright coloured paintings.

Leah admired a hair barrette decorated with white, blue and purple beaded flowers.

"All this is made by the Siksika people." A man in a black cowboy hat trimmed with intricate beadwork stepped out from behind a counter. "Oh—hi there. You're Dan's friends, aren't you? I'm Ed Crow Feather. We met at the Cowboy Boot Warehouse."

"Hiya. Yes, I'm Amanda and this is my friend, Leah. We would like to see some of your work."

"That's one of my paintings over there." He pointed to a picture of a black eagle, silhouetted against a red background. "But mostly I do carvings. Come to the back, and I'll show you what I'm working on right now."

Ed led the girls into a back room filled with an assortment of tools and chunks of stone. In the middle of the room, on a table, sat a large eagle partially carved out of granite.

"Wow! This is awesome. It looks so real. May I touch it?" asked Amanda.

"Of course."

The stone felt smooth and cool as she ran her hand over the eagle's head and down its back.

"You are very good. The feathers look so real!" Amanda noticed a bowl of stones sitting on a shelf beside the carving. Some with marks on them. "What do those marks mean?"

"Oh, those. They mean nothing." Ed picked up the bowl and put it on a top shelf.

Amanda would have liked to look at the stones more closely. She wondered what he was trying to hide.

Leah held a small carving in her hand. "Is this a dog?"

"No, that is a coyote." Ed laughed. "Do you know why the coyote howls at the stars at night?"

The girls both shook their heads.

"Well, I will tell you. Legend has it that coyote was just being coyote when he saw the Creator placing the stars in the sky from a bag in a very orderly manner. Coyote asked if he could help and the Creator let coyote place stars in the sky, reminding him to be sure and put the stars up in an orderly manner. Coyote did it correctly, but, as is his nature, coyote became impatient and threw the whole bag of stars into the sky distributing the stars helter skelter. The Creator scolded him for his carelessness and for the mess he made. Now, coyote howls at night when he looks up and sees the mess he made with the stars."

"That's such a cool story. Thanks for telling it to us." Leah purchased the coyote carving for her mom and the beaded barrette for herself.

As they left the shop, the girls spotted Dan in a heated discussion with Andy Rowlands in the middle of the boardwalk. Both men appeared angry. Andy poked his middle finger at Dan's chest. They couldn't hear what he was saying as his back was to them.

"Leave my uncle alone. He doesn't know where it is, I tell you." They heard Dan shout.

Andy turned around and saw Amanda and Leah. He pushed his hat to the back of his head and broke into a broad smile. "Well, if it isn't the heroes of the day. How is your great-aunt?"

"She's doing great. We just saw her this morning," replied Amanda.

Dan spotted the gift shop bag. "I see you found my uncle's studio. I'm sure he was pleased to see both of you."

"Leah bought something for herself and for her mom and your uncle showed us the carving of an eagle he's working on. It's so awesome. He also had some stones with carvings on them like the ones you have on the ranch, Andy. I sure wish I knew what those marks mean."

Andy glared at Dan. Dan glanced at Amanda with dark eyes.

"They're just some old stones that don't mean anything." Dan tipped his hat. "Enjoy the rest of your visit."

"Oh, we will. We're going to Head-Smashed-In Buffalo Jump tomorrow." Amanda replied.

With a scowl on his face, Dan turned and stomped away.

CHAPTER 9

"Are we still going to Head-Smashed-In Buffalo Jump, Mom?" Amanda asked the next morning.

"I still have a couple of days off so I thought it would be a fun day trip. Sorry, Leah, no stores for you, but it is interesting."

"I'm actually loving all this prairie stuff that I didn't know about before. I just find castles and old cathedrals so very dull." Leah pulled her hair back in a low ponytail. "I suppose that's because I'm surrounded by them all the time."

"That's so funny. I've always thought the prairies were boring." Amanda reached for the cowboy hats and two bottles of water. "Looks like another scorcher. Glad we have A-C in the SUV."

Soon after they left the city they passed a herd of large, shaggy, dark brown animals, each with a hump on its shoulders, grazing in a field.

"Are those really...bison?" asked Leah. "I thought they were all extinct."

"They almost were, but some ranchers are raising

them now and slowly increasing the herds. They will never be as numerous as they once were though." Mrs. Ross pulled over to the side of the road. "Would you like to take some pictures?"

Leah took a few shots. Then she stood in front of the barbed wire fence while Amanda took pictures of her and the bison roaming behind her.

"My mates back home will love this photo. I'll post it on Instagram tonight."

Ω Ω Ω

An hour later, they stopped at an interpretive centre in the middle of the prairie.

"Wowza! Is it ever hot here," said Leah as she got out of the air conditioned jeep. "There isn't a tree in sight for shade either. It's like the UAE." She quickly put on her cowboy hat.

"Yup," replied Amanda. "It can get up to forty degrees Celsius here in the summer. But it can also go down to minus forty in the winter."

"Oh, I couldn't handle the cold." Leah shivered in spite of the heat.

"You just bundle up, that's all." Amanda took a sip of water.

"Are you girls going to stand around and talk about the weather or are we going to see the sights?" asked Amanda's mother.

They entered a building built right into the cliff, the same beige colour of the sandstone and rocks surrounding it. Inside, they followed the signs of the small red buffalo directing them to the seven levels of displays. Amanda and Leah were intrigued as they read the storyboards explaining the geography, climate and native people of the area and of the buffalo hunt itself.

They stopped to listen to a man who introduced himself as a member of the Blackfoot Confederacy. He explained how his ancestors used their knowledge of buffalo behaviour and the terrain to their benefit.

While he talked, he pointed to the series of murals showing the stages of a buffalo hunt. The first picture showed how young men, disguised under animal hides, lured the herds towards the cliffs. He called them the Buffalo Runners.

The crowd of listeners kept growing as he continued his talk. "Other tribe members, mainly women and children, hid behind stone cairns, placed to create a V path to the cliff's edge. They would shout and wave buffalo hides to keep the animals on the track."

The series of pictures showed clearly how effective the technique was. "Hunters ran behind the herd, further frightening the animals. At last, the buffalo plunged over the cliff to their death on the valley floor. This was how a tribe could obtain a large amount of food in a short time."

He chuckled. "In those days we didn't have Super-store. Without the buffalo hunt the people would not survive the long winters." The crowd laughed at his joke.

"My, they were ever so clever," commented Leah.

"Yes, they were," said the man. "There was little waste too. Almost every part of the animal was used." He handed a crude version of a spoon to Leah. "For instance, this spoon was made from the horn of a bison."

Amanda picked up another item. "I guess this would have been a hammer."

"You're right. They used those hammers to pound the animal skins to make them soft."

She became lost in examining the bone handle with a rock tied onto it by a tightly wrapped leather cord. She felt someone near her and looked up.

A cowboy leaned in close to her and said in a harsh whisper, "Be careful how you handle the artifacts." His steely grey eyes fixed on her for a few moments and then he moved away. Amanda searched to see where he had gone, but her view of the exits was blocked by other people in the room.

Leah continued talking to the guide, asking questions. Amanda put her hand on her friend's shoulder to get her attention. "D-did you see the guy who was just standing here?"

"No, I didn't see anyone. But I was busy looking at

these old tools."

Mrs. Ross appeared and suggested they go to the top floor where there was a lookout.

At the top of the cliff, the girls gazed over the rail at the sweeping sage-green prairie. They noticed the remnants of the rocks piled up to create cairns thousands of years ago. A guide explained that this historic site was older than the pyramids in Egypt or Stonehenge in England. He pointed out the spot where the bison tumbled over the cliff. A hot, dry wind blew across the plateau. Amanda imagined the frightened, huge beasts thundering along unaware of their fate, and she felt sad.

The guide showed them the tipis set up in the valley below, ready for the butchering. He described how once the animals were skinned and cut into chunks, the parts were taken back to the campsite for storage. He then invited everyone to walk down to the valley along a trail if they wished.

"You girls can check it out if you like." Mrs. Ross blotted her face with a tissue. "It's too hot. I'm going to the café for an iced tea. Meet me there later."

Leah and Amanda followed the guide down a path that led to the bottom of the cliff.

"Is it called Head-Smashed-In Buffalo Jump because the animals smashed their heads when they went over the cliff?" asked Leah.

"Legend has it that a young boy wanted to get a good look at the buffalo as they went over the cliff. He stood too close and a buffalo fell on top of him smashing in his head. The people then called it Head-Smashed-In."

"Maybe the parents used the story to warn other children not to get too close," remarked Amanda.

"Perhaps." The guide nodded. "Many of our legends have a lesson in them."

Soon they came upon some tipis in a circle. The tops were painted with black dots and stripes and a single huge buffalo decorated each side.

While Leah continued to ask the guide questions, Amanda examined the nearest tipi. She looked to see if she could spot any more symbols similar to the one on the rock. She ended up around the back of the tent when the same cowboy appeared.

"Where is the stone?"

"I...I don't know what you're talking about."

"Yes, you do." The cowboy put both hands on her shoulders. "I heard you have the stone and I want it!" He began to shake her.

Amanda stepped back. The cowboy moved forward. She took another step back, tripped in a gopher hole and fell flat on her back. The cowboy fell on top of her.

"If you know what's good fer you, you'll hand over that stone to me," he growled through his yellowed teeth.

His breath smelt of stale cigarette smoke and onions. Amanda held her breath.

A hand came around the cowboy's throat and pulled him back. His hat fell to the ground, revealing curly ginger hair.

"Leave her alone, Hank. She doesn't have anything to do with this."

Amanda looked up and saw Dan with the cowboy firmly in his grip. Leah stood behind him with her eyes wide and her mouth open as if she wanted to say something but couldn't get the words out.

Hank struggled to free himself from Dan's hold, picked up his hat and slammed it against his leg before plunking it on his head. He stared hard at Amanda and strode away.

Amanda trembled as Leah and Dan helped her up.

"Are you OK?" asked Leah.

"Boy, am I glad you guys showed up when you did."

"I wanted to tell you Dan was here, but I couldn't find you. We heard a noise and came back here to find you being attacked by that awful man. What did he want?"

"I...I don't know," stammered Amanda as she brushed dirt and dry grass off her arms and legs.

CHAPTER 10

Perhaps we should go back to the café, Amanda. We've been gone for some time and your mom might be worried," said a concerned Leah.

"A good idea. I feel a bit weird. I need a cold drink and my water bottle is empty." Amanda turned to Dan. "Would you like to join us?"

"I think I will. I wouldn't want that ranch hand bothering you again."

"Isn't he the guy who got in a fight with your uncle at the Bar U Ranch?"

"I don't know. I wasn't there." Dan shrugged as he surveyed the area.

"Shouldn't we report what happened?" asked Leah.

"I'd rather not," said Amanda. "I don't want my mom to know what happened. She'll just get upset."

"It's probably best," agreed Dan. "Though I'd steer clear of Hank and Andy and those fellows at the ranch if I were you."

Ω Ω Ω

Mrs. Ross looked up from her cell phone and smiled when she saw the girls and Dan enter the café. "You all look like you could use some iced tea?"

"Oh yes, please," said Dan and Amanda at the same time.

"I'll have a lemonade, if that's OK," said Leah. "I'm just not into cold tea."

"Don't you drink iced tea in England?" asked Dan.

"Not usually, we prefer hot tea."

Dan helped Amanda's mom bring the drinks to the table.

"I just received a text from Uncle Jimmy saying that Great Aunt Mary has been released from the hospital. Perhaps we can stop at her house on our way home."

"That would be awesome." Amanda took a long drink and then said, "What brings you to Head-Smashed-In Buffalo Jump today, Dan?"

"You mentioned yesterday that you were planning to come out here. It's been a long time since I visited this place. I had the day off so I decided to take a drive out here." Dan finished his drink. "Thanks for the tea, Mrs. Ross. I best get going." He looked at Amanda and Leah. "Take it easy, eh. Don't talk to any strangers." He winked.

Amanda wondered what he meant by that remark.

"Leah, you hardly touched your drink. What's wrong with it?"

Leah scrunched up her nose. "When I asked for lemonade, I thought I was getting a fizzy drink."

"Oh, that's right. I forgot. In England, the lemonade is like a ginger ale or a sprite. Sorry, Leah." Amanda gave her friend a hug.

Ω Ω Ω

Unusually quiet, Leah and Amanda barely spoke in the van until they got to the city. Aunt Mary lived in an older house near the Bow River. Filled with artifacts from travels with her late husband, it smelled like old books and lavender. Her home had a real cozy feeling.

"How kind of you to stop in, Evelyn. They couldn't wait to kick me out of that hospital. They don't keep you in very long these days. Just as well, the food's terrible. What did you think of Head-Smashed-In, Leah?"

"It was grand, thank you," said Leah. "It was like being in an American Western. I learned so much about things I hadn't known before."

"I've been going out to that site for years, long before it became a UNESCO World Heritage Site. I've found some interesting arrowheads and tools. Donated them back to the museum of course."

"Aunt Mary has a lovely garden out the back. Would you like to have a look at it, Leah?" asked Mrs. Ross.

While Leah and Amanda's mom checked out the garden, Amanda took the opportunity to ask her great aunt some questions about petroglyphs.

"I have a book for you. It's there on the shelf," said her aunt.

Amanda picked up a book with pictures of interesting rock carvings on the cover.

"Do you still have that stone you told me about?"

"Yes, and I haven't told anyone else about it. Not even Leah. Do you think it might be important?"

"Well, it might be. Perhaps you should bring it with you the next time you come for a visit, so I can have a look at it."

Amanda was tempted to tell her about the incident at Head-Smashed-In, but thought better of it.

Ω Ω Ω

Later that night as they got ready for bed, Leah plunked her hands on her hips and turned to Amanda.

"What actually happened today? Do you realize what a fright you gave me? What if we hadn't shown up? What are you not telling me?"

Amanda sighed. It was time to confess.

"At the parade something fell out of the clown's pocket and I picked it up." She walked over to her bookshelf and picked up the stone. "It was this." She placed the stone in Leah's hand. "I didn't think it was important, but now everyone seems to want it."

Leah ran her thumb over the smooth stone and

traced the mark. "I wonder what this means?"

Amanda reached in her backpack and pulled out the book Aunt Mary gave her. "Maybe this book will help us figure it out."

Leah looked at her friend. "Honestly, Amanda, is this what the cowboy wanted from you? Is that why he had you pinned to the ground?"

"Well, he didn't actually push me down. I moved back to get away from him and tripped in a gopher hole. That's when he fell on top of me. It probably looked worse than it was and he actually seemed embarrassed. He demanded I tell him where the stone was. I have no idea how he knew I had it in the first place."

"It looks like you've got yourself in a pickle, again." Leah shook her head. "Let's look through this book. Maybe it will give us a clue as to why anyone would want a silly old stone so badly."

The book was full of fascinating rock carvings from all over North America. Amanda turned to a section on Canadian Aboriginal Art and Culture and read out loud, "In the past the Plains Indians didn't have a written alphabet so they passed on their history and stories by painting images on bison hides and painting or carving pictures on rocks."

"Look at these amazing petroglyphs pecked into the rocks. They kind of look like kid's drawings, don't they?"

Leah looked over Amanda's shoulder. "Do you think that is supposed to be a buffalo? And perhaps those are the buffalo tracks."

They both looked closely at the picture.

Amanda said, "They could be tracks, I guess. The marks look a bit like a horseshoe but more like a 'v' than a 'u'."

Leah looked at the smooth rock in her hand with the faint impression of a V.

"Do you think this piece of rock could be part of a larger drawing telling a story?"

"Perhaps, and maybe it's valuable." Amanda took the stone from Leah and gently stroked it as she wondered how old it might be. "I think it's time we consulted Great Aunt Mary. She'll know what to do."

Chapter 11

"Mooom! Why do we have to get up so early on summer holidays?" Amanda rubbed her eyes as she looked at the clock beside her bed.

"I have to go in to work. Uncle Jimmy just called and you've been invited to go on a cattle drive at the Bar U Ranch. Your cousin Gordon is picking you up in thirty minutes. Now, get a move on."

Amanda and Leah looked at each other.

"Well, I wanted to go visit Aunt Mary today. I have something to ask her. Plus, I thought you said you had a couple of days off."

"I did, but they need me today so I have to go in. Whatever it is, you can wait to ask Aunt Mary another time. For heaven's sake, Amanda, I thought you would be happy to go on a cattle drive. What a great experience for Leah. How many young girls from England can say they've been on a real cattle drive?"

As Mrs. Ross left the girls to get ready, she said, "Wear jeans and long sleeves. It's a bit cooler today and there may be mosquitoes."

"It looks like we're going on a cattle drive." Amanda jumped out of bed.

"What about that mean ranch hand?" Leah asked as she braided her hair.

"We'll just keep clear of him. Besides, there will be lots of other people around. We'll be OK."

Soon a pickup truck pulled up in front of the house, and a tall, lanky, young man swung down from the cab. He pushed his cowboy hat to the back of his head and said, "I hear you city slickers need a ride to a cattle drive. You sure you can handle the tough life of a wrangler?" He grinned from ear to ear.

"Stop teasing, Gordon. We can hold our own." Amanda punched her cousin's shoulder.

"Ya, right. I brought Sarah along, just to be sure."

The girls climbed into the cab, squishing in beside Sarah.

Ω Ω Ω

A hive of activity greeted them upon arrival at the ranch. Restless cows mooed. Horses whinnied, swishing their tails as they trotted back and forth along the fence. Eager cowboys and cowgirls shouted to each other. Bart barked with excitement.

Andy, dressed in a long, brown oilskin coat and a black cowboy hat, strode over to the half-ton truck. "Howdy. Glad to see you decided to join us today on our annual cattle drive. We don't have as many cattle as we used to, but they still need to be moved to another pasture. Are you joining us, Gord?"

"Sorry, Dad needs me on the farm today. We've started the baling. I'll pick these three up at four o'clock," answered Gordon.

"Don't you worry none. I'll see they're looked after." Andy patted the window frame with the palms of his hands.

The girls piled out of the truck and Gordon drove away in a cloud of dust.

"Follow me to the saddle horse barn so we can get you saddled up and ready." Andy and Bart led the way.

The barn smelled of fresh hay. Amanda noticed Leah's nose twitch and remembered that she suffered from hay fever.

"Will you be OK?" she asked her friend.

"I'll be fine once we get outside and away from this stuff." Leah sniffed.

Soon all three girls rode their horses beside the noisy cows as they headed out of the yard. They had been instructed to watch out for any strays. It was important to keep the herd together. All the cows had the Bar U brand on them so it was easy to know if they belonged.

The cattle came in all shapes and sizes; most were chocolate brown but a few were black with white faces. Amanda loved the young ones. She thought they were just so cute. The cows stirred up a cloud of dust as they stomped along the dry prairie road swishing flies off their backs with their tails.

"What was that?" asked Leah pointing to a small furry animal that dashed across the trail in front of them and dove into a hole in the ground.

"Oh, that was a gopher," said Sarah. "We've got plenty of them around here. Watch and you might see him come out of another hole."

"Oh, look! There he is!" shouted Leah as she pointed to a tiny brown head popping out of an opening in the ground further down the way. "How did he get over there?"

"Their underground home is actually a network of tunnels with many openings," explained Sarah.

"Hey, you girls! Pay attention. Didn't you see that youngster stray? You best get him back over here," a ranch hand shouted from the other side of the herd.

A black calf headed toward the trees. Sarah turned her horse in the direction of the runaway. Amanda and Leah followed. The little guy appeared to be happy to get away from the grown-ups and moved at a good speed. Once in the forest the girls lost sight of him.

"Where did he go?" Amanda looked from left to right.

"I think he's over there." Leah pointed to movement in the trees. As they got closer, no calf appeared.

Sarah stopped her horse and looked around. "That's odd. It's as if he just disappeared into thin air."

A twig snapped.

"What was that?" Amanda squirmed in her saddle.

The forest was silent for a moment and then a slender, beige deer-like animal jumped out from behind a tree and skipped away through the pines.

"It was just an antelope." Sarah laughed with relief. "Now where did that crazy little runaway get to?"

The girls rode through the tall trees keeping a sharp eye out until they came upon a clearing with a small cabin. The windows were boarded over and the door hung open on one hinge.

"Do you think the calf got in there?" asked Leah.

The girls dismounted. They peered in through the door at a dim, gloomy room. A tree branch had found its way in between the window frame. A table, set with tin plates and cups, sat in the middle of the dirt floor waiting for the owners to come home for dinner. Cobwebs and dust covered everything.

Amanda shuddered. "This place gives me the creeps. I think we should turn back."

"This what you're lookin' fer?"

A cowboy in a long, dark-brown oilskin coat came around the corner of the shack pulling an unhappy black calf. Amanda's heart skipped a beat when she recognized him as Hank.

"Yes," she said. "We need to get him back to the herd. What are you doing with him anyway?"

"Don't you worry. I'll see he gets back with his momma. But your cattle drive is over." He wrapped the rope around a tree and walked up to the girls in the doorway. "Get in the hut."

The girls didn't move.

"I said, git in the hut. Now!"

Hank shoved Sarah and Leah, who fell against Amanda and they all tumbled onto the dirt floor of the abandoned shack. Hank slammed the door shut.

"Maybe you will think about who you'll give that stone to while you spend time in there," he shouted as he hammered a board across the door.

Amanda could hear the frightened calf bawl as Hank led him away. 'He better not hurt that calf,' she thought as her eyes became accustomed to the dark.

Chapter 12

Specks of dust danced in a sliver of light shining through an opening by a boarded up window. The stale air smelled musty. No one had been in the cabin for some time. Thick dust covered the sparse furniture.

Leah sat up and picked her hat off the dirt floor. "WTG, Amanda. Now, what have you got us into? Why don't you just give him the stupid rock?"

"What are you talking about?" asked Sarah as she brushed dust off her jeans. "What rock? And what does WTG mean anyway?"

"Way to go. Amanda found a rock with a weird mark on it. Somehow, certain people know she has it and are trying to get it from her. This Hank guy is scary."

Amanda studied the window. "I think the important thing right now is finding a way out of this place. I don't know about you guys, but I don't want to stay in here for any longer than I have to. Who knows what creepy crawlies are in here—or worse."

She shuddered as she walked over to the window. Her fingers just fit in the small opening, blocking out the only light in the shack. A tug at the window frame, and the old dry wood broke away. She pulled at another piece with the same result.

"Come on you guys; help pull this wood away to give us more light in here."

While Leah and Sarah pulled more of the window frame away, Amanda spotted a cast iron frying pan hanging on the wall. After brushing away cobwebs, she lifted it off the hook. It weighed a ton.

"Move out of the way!" she shouted.

With both hands, she lifted the heavy pan in the air and smashed the boards covering the window. The wood gave way allowing in bright sunlight along with the fresh smell of evergreens.

Amanda grinned at the other girls, "Easy peasy. Now, let's get out of here."

Leah climbed out first since she had the longest legs. Then she helped Sarah and Amanda make the short jump to the ground.

"Where are our horses?" Amanda looked around. "Don't tell me Hank took the horses."

"It looks like we'll be walking," said Leah. "I hope one of you knows the way out of this forest."

Sarah pointed toward an opening in the trees. "I think we came in that way."

After walking for a few minutes, Leah began to sneeze.

"Are you OK, Leah?" asked Amanda.

"It was awfully dusty in that shack. I could use some water, but I guess the canteens went with the horses." Leah sighed.

"I'm sorry, Leah." Amanda felt bad.

Sarah pointed to movement in the trees ahead. "What's that?"

"Oh no. I hope it's not Hank coming back. Let's hide behind this big tree," whispered Amanda.

All three girls scrunched together. Amanda peeked around the trunk. A man in a long dark coat and black hat walked toward the tree. He looked at the ground so she couldn't see his face. Amanda ducked back.

'It's got to be Hank,' she thought. Her heart pounded so loud she was sure the man could hear it as he got closer to the tree. Leah pressed against her. Amanda could feel her shaking. Sarah leaned on Leah and squeezed her elbows tight against her sides, trying to be as small as possible.

Footsteps crunched on the forest floor coming closer and closer to the tree. Amanda held her breath and willed her heart to stop pounding. Then the footsteps began to sound further away. Amanda peered around the tree again. The man was walking away from the tree. She relaxed and started to breathe again.

Just when he was a comfortable distance away, Leah sneezed. Amanda stopped breathing. "I'm so sorry,"

Leah mouthed.

The man stopped and turned toward the tree. At the same time there was a rustle in the brush and a barking dog emerged. Bart ran right up to the tree wagging his tail in excitement.

"Have you found them, Bart? That's a good boy. You're not just good for rounding up cattle, but missing girls as well." Andy let out a huge breath as he came around the tree. "Are you young ones OK? You gave us quite a scare when your horses turned up without you. Why are you hiding behind this tree?"

"W-we thought you were Hank. He, he took our horses after he locked us in an old cabin," gasped Amanda still giddy with fright.

"Hank? Hank McGavity? You mean the ranch hand that used to work for me?" Andy removed his hat and scratched his head. "He's nowhere around these parts. Last I heard he went to work on a ranch in Saskatchewan after I fired him. He's nothing but a trouble maker, that one. He wouldn't dare turn up here."

"I'm pretty sure it was Hank," said Amanda, regaining her composure. "He had red hair."

Andy shook his head. "Now why would Hank want to lock you in a cabin and take your horses?" He put his hat back on. "We need to get you girls back to the ranch, fed and watered before Gord comes back to pick you up."

Amanda had a feeling Andy didn't believe their story. She was relieved he had found them though.

Andy led the way back through the trees to the road and then drove the shaken girls to the ranch in his truck. Once there, they were given cold drinks and roast beef sandwiches in the cookhouse. The cook pulled out a batch of fresh baked cookies from the oven. The girls soon felt better.

"If you young ladies are all right now, I best be joining the cattle drive. They should be almost at the other pasture by now." Andy got up to leave.

"Can't we join the rest of the cattle drive too?" asked Amanda.

"No way. You've had enough excitement for one day, Missy. Besides, I promised Gord I would look after you girls, and a man's word is a man's word." Andy wrinkled his brow. "Cook here will look after you. Just let her know if you need anything." He motioned to the sleeping dog, "Come along, Bart."

Andy and Bart jumped in the half ton and drove away, leaving a trail of dust.

"Now what are we going to do until my brother gets here?" asked Sarah.

"Let's go up to the bunkhouse." Amanda headed toward the stairs. "I think I saw some stones up there when we were here last time, and I'd like to check them out."

"Not more stones, Amanda." Leah shook her head. "Isn't that what just got us locked in a horrible old shack?" She looked over at Sarah, shrugged her shoulders and followed Amanda up the stairs.

Everything looked as it did when they first visited.

"I guess this isn't where the cowboys actually sleep," remarked Leah.

"No," said Sarah. "This is a museum which shows you what it was like a long time ago."

Amanda looked around but couldn't see any stones on the bedside table where she had spotted them before.

A loud thump came from downstairs.

"Hey, you! Get out of my kitchen, you good-for-nothing. I thought Mr. Rowlands told you to get lost." The screen door slammed.

The girls looked out the window to see a man with red hair sprinting across the field. The cook ran behind him with her broom in the air. She stopped when he jumped in the creek and waded to the bushes on the other side.

"And don't you think of coming back! You hear?" She waved her broom above her head, spun around and returned to the cookhouse.

The girls ran down the stairs.

"Is everything all right?" asked Amanda as the cook entered the kitchen, her face red and her hair disheveled.

The frazzled woman placed the broom by the old stove and smoothed down her apron. "That Hank McGavity has been nothing but trouble since he was a young boy. Mr. Rowlands was kind enough to give him a job here but he kept getting into fights with the other ranch hands. He's a good bronco rider, although he's had a string of bad luck lately at the rodeos. He's always short of cash. Not sure what he does with his earnings. He ain't got no horse sense."

"What was he doing here?" asked Leah.

"Darned if I know. He was told never to return when he was fired last week. He gave me quite a fright when I opened the pantry and found him hiding behind the butter churn." The cook's hand trembled as she tidied her hair.

Just then a half ton truck pulled up.

"It's my brother." Sarah looked relieved.

"Had enough cattle driving?" Gordon slammed the truck door. "Almost picked up a hitchhiker but I was going the wrong way. Guy looked a sorry sight. Looked a lot like Hank McGavity, come to think of it." He shook his head. "But I heard he's gone from these parts."

Amanda looked at Leah and Sarah. No one said a thing.

Chapter 13

"Y̲ou girls sure are quiet," said Gordon as they rattled along the road. "Cat got your tongue?"

Sarah shrugged her shoulders. "We're just tired, that's all."

"Hope you don't mind some music then." Gordon turned on the radio and tapped his hands on the steering wheel to country and western tunes for the rest of the trip back to the city.

Amanda's mom arrived home from work just as the weary travellers drove up. She invited Gordon and Sarah in for a snack.

"Sorry, Aunt Evelyn, but we have to get back to the farm to do the chores. Dad's busy in the fields baling hay right now, and Mom needs our help."

"Thanks for driving the girls to the ranch and back, Gordon. Say hi to your mom and dad." She turned to Amanda and Leah. "You two look like you could use a shower and an early night. Tomorrow we're driving to Drumheller. Do you like dinosaurs, Leah?"

Ω Ω Ω

The next morning, while getting dressed, Amanda noticed the stone on her bookshelf. She picked it up, examined it closely and thought, 'I wonder why Hank wants this stone so badly. What does it mean? Why did Ed have it in his pocket the day of the parade? If only I could talk to Aunt Mary about it.'

"Penny for your thoughts?" Leah appeared behind her.

Amanda slipped the stone in her jeans pocket. "Nothing...really."

"I'm glad we'll be far away from the ranch and all that. I don't imagine dead dinosaurs will be interested in silly old rocks." Leah flashed a smile.

"Gosh, I'm glad you're not mad about what happened yesterday."

"Now it just seems like a silly old dream." Leah raised her eyebrows and rolled her eyes. "Life is never dull with you, Amanda."

Ω Ω Ω

The drive to Drumheller took them past endless flat fields of pale golden wheat. Cows grazed in green pastures, kept safely from the traffic by prickly barbed wire fences. Giant rocking pump jacks dotted the countryside taking oil out of the ground. They looked like nodding donkeys.

"We call those, cow-chow," said Amanda as she

pointed to a field of round bales that looked like steam-rollers.

Leah giggled. "What is that?" She pointed in the distance to a bright yellow streak that looked as if someone had run a highlighter over the land.

"That's a canola field," answered Mrs. Ross. "Canola is grown for its oil. The plant is a bright yellow like that when it's in full bloom, ready to be harvested. The 'can' part stands for Canada and 'ola' refers to oil. Canola is grown primarily here, in the prairies of Western Canada."

"You sound like an encyclopaedia, Mom."

"I live and work in the city, but I grew up on a farm. My dad taught me all this stuff. I thought Leah would like to know, that's all."

Soon the wheat fields gave way to rugged hills with flat tops, layered like a cake in various shades of brown, beige and grey.

"Now that we can see the badlands, we're almost at Drumheller," said Mrs. Ross.

"Why are they called badlands? Do bad people live there, like outlaws?" asked Leah.

Amanda laughed, "We don't have outlaws here anymore. That's just in the movies."

"It's true, outlaws used to hide in the badlands. Horsethief Canyon is so-named because it was used by American horse thieves in the old west for hiding stolen horses to sell in Alberta," answered Amanda's mom. "As for the name badlands, apparently the French-Canadian trappers used to call them *mauvaises terres pour traverser,* which means 'bad lands to cross'."

"I forgot that you speak French here in Canada," said Leah.

"We learn it in school but many of us aren't fluent, especially here in Western Canada." Mrs. Ross turned into a town nestled between the badlands.

"OMG! What is that!" Leah pointed to a looming Tyrannosaurus Rex in the distance. "Is that the dinosaur museum?"

"No, we're not at the museum yet. That's just an oversized replica by the Visitor Information Centre."

As they drove into town they noticed dinosaurs of all sizes and colours everywhere they looked: on signs, in front of shops, in the playgrounds and on street corners.

"Look at that cute one!" Amanda pointed to a pink creature with purple polka dots.

"This sure is a dinosaur town," said Leah. "Look at that one painted white with red horns and red maple leaves on its side."

They pulled up in front of the Visitor Information Centre. *The World's Largest Dinosaur* stared down at them. His mammoth mouth opened wide displaying sharp teeth. People looked out of his mouth as if he just had them for lunch.

"I just need to stop in here for a minute," said Mrs. Ross.

"And I need to take a picture of this monster." Leah pulled out her camera. "My mates back home won't ever believe this."

"Can we go inside the dinosaur, Mom? It says on the sign we can and it doesn't cost much," Amanda asked when her mom returned to the car.

"Not now, maybe on the way back. I'll drive you to the museum to look around while I drop off some paperwork at a client's office. He's expecting me soon."

The Royal Tyrrell Museum sat in a valley surrounded by badlands. Greeting visitors at the entrance stood replicas of Triceratops. A sign explained that the name meant three-horns-on-the-face.

"One, two, three." Leah touched each horn as she counted. "The perfect name for him."

"Look at the babies by this one. She must be a mommy Triceratops." Amanda shouted. "They are super cute!"

"I'll see you in two hours at this entrance," said Mrs. Ross. She waved out the window as she drove away.

The girls entered the museum behind a group of children, led by a nurse. Some of the children were in wheelchairs. A couple of them had no hair. Amanda thought one girl in the group looked familiar.

They entered a dark hall with a swampy smell. Four life-sized replicas of dinosaurs, with massive heads and dozens of sharp teeth, were displayed in a dry riverbed. They stood about eleven feet tall and thirty feet long, with long thick tails and tiny useless arms. A sign explained the dinosaurs were called Albertosaurus, which meant Alberta Lizard.

"This is what Alberta looked like 70 million years ago," read Amanda.

"Scary. Glad I wasn't around back then. Imagine running into one of these." Leah grimaced as she stared at a huge beast baring his teeth, ready to take a bite out of her.

Amanda took a picture of Leah in front of the enormous creatures. Then they took a couple of selfies making faces as if they were about to be eaten alive.

They moved on into another gallery called Dinosaur Hall, full of skeletons of dinosaurs that had been unearthed in the area.

"This is totally brilliant," exclaimed Leah. "Did they really dig up these bones here?"

"You bet. Look at this one called Black Beauty; it's the head of a Tyrannosaurus Rex found by a couple of teenagers."

"How exciting would that be if we were to find dinosaur bones!" Leah's eyes sparkled.

Against one wall, beside a ruler, hung the skeleton of

a dinosaur foot. The sign under it said:

HOW DO YOU MEASURE UP?

The group of children with the nurse took turns standing beside the foot to see how tall they were in comparison. One boy measured five feet and barely passed the first joint past the toes of the dinosaur.

Amanda and Leah waited their turn. A First Nations girl smiled at them as she walked up to be measured. Amanda smiled back and wished she could remember where she had seen her before.

A guide began a presentation. The children crowded around him as he explained about the dinosaurs and how they were discovered. The man held a rock six inches long and four inches wide, flat at the bottom and curved at the top. He asked the group if they knew what it was. He handed it around for everyone to examine. No one could guess.

Amanda asked, "Could it be a toe?"

"You are right! It is a toe from a T-Rex."

"If the toe was this big, imagine the rest of him." Leah shuddered.

The same young girl smiled at them again. "Do you remember me? You watched me at the Pow-wow when I did the Jingle Dress Dance."

"That's right. You're Dan's sister, Sharon." Amanda grinned. "I didn't recognize you without your Jingle

Dress Dance outfit. What are you doing here?"

"The hospital arranged for all of us in our ward to go on an outing. We got to pick where we wanted to go for a day and we chose this museum. I love learning all about dinosaurs, don't you? You were clever to guess the stone was actually a petrified dinosaur toe."

The nurse waiting with the rest of the children motioned to Sharon.

"I must go and join the others. It was good to see you guys again. Hope you have a nice time here in Alberta, Leah. It's a cool place isn't it?"

"Oh yes, it's totally amazing. There is an awful lot to see and do."

Sharon ran over to the other kids from the hospital, turned and waved.

"She sure is nice." Amanda waved back and then turned to Leah. "I wonder why she's in the hospital."

CHAPTER 14

The girls proceeded from one room to the next taking in all the amazing artifacts, fossils, bones and entire skeletons found in the area. Each discovery had a story. They stopped in front of a window displaying a small, complete skeleton embedded in a rock.

Amanda read from the display board under the window. "It says here this was a young, swift-running, long-legged dinosaur called a Gorgosaurus."

"Why is its head flung back almost touching its tail?" asked Leah.

"Apparently this is what is called the classic death pose." Amanda scrunched her nose as she read. "The poor thing died like this."

Nimble raptors, with killer claws perched on top of pedestals, followed the girls with stony eyes as they walked by. Skeletons of slow moving Stegosaurus with bony plates on their backs and four lethal spikes in each tail, stood beside duck-billed Edmontosaurus and three horned Triceratops. A Dimetrodon with a huge sail on its back was dwarfed by the gigantic Tyrannosaurus Rex in the centre of the room.

"Can you believe these things used to roam this very area!" Amanda exclaimed.

Leah continued to snap pictures. "I have never, ever, seen anything like this."

A young palaeontologist with a small pointed knife that looked like an old fountain pen meticulously chipped bits of stone away from a recently unearthed bone. The girls stopped to watch.

Amanda noticed a sign under a bone in a case that read: *Discovered by Mary Johnson, 1997.*

"Look at this, Leah." She pointed to the sign. "This dinosaur bone was discovered by my great aunt Mary."

Leah took a picture with Amanda pointing at the sign.

The young palaeontologist put down his tool and said, "Mrs. Johnson is your great aunt?"

"Yes," said Amanda. "She's my mom's aunt; my grandma's sister."

"I was honoured to be mentored by Mrs. Johnson during my studies at the University of Calgary. I learned more from her than I did from the courses I took. She sure knows her stuff."

"She loves fossils and dinosaur bones and things, that's for sure." Amanda thought for a minute and then pulled the stone out of her pocket. "You wouldn't know anything about the mark on this stone."

The young man took it from her and held it close to one eye. "This is interesting. It could be the footprint of a small dinosaur but I think it's more likely a petroglyph. It could be part of a larger picture. That's not really my field of study." He wrinkled his brow. "Where did you get this? You are aware that it is illegal to take any fossils or artifacts you find around here?"

"Y-yah, I know. I didn't really find it. It found me." Amanda's face turned red.

"Perhaps you should take it to the office and turn it in. It could be very important and also valuable. Does Mrs. Johnson know about this?"

The young man directed the girls to the office and returned to his chore.

As Amanda and Leah approached the door it swung open, almost knocking them over. An older gentleman in a tweed suit barged out of a large room full of papers and boxes piled up everywhere. Following him was a man in a cowboy hat.

Amanda's mouth fell open when she recognized Andy Rowlands. 'What is he doing here,' she wondered.

Unaware of their presence, Andy said, "I only need a few more pieces and then I can bring the entire set to show you. I will be willing to sell them to the museum for a fair price. I figure you'll be mighty impressed when you see what I've stumbled upon."

"We will want Mary Johnson to look it over first.

She's the expert in these parts when it comes to that sort of thing. No decision will be made without her approval."

"Fair enough." Andy shook the gentleman's hand and strode off.

The man returned to his office and closed the door without noticing the two girls behind it.

"Well, aren't you going to go in and give the stone to that man?" asked Leah.

Amanda shook her head. "No, I really think I need to show it to Aunt Mary first. Something just doesn't seem right. I wonder what Mr. Rowlands was talking about?"

"I think you're making a big thing of it. I figure you should hand it over to the museum and then no one will be trying to get it from you anymore. Remember, just yesterday we were locked in a smelly old cabin and left for dead?"

"I've got to think about it. I'm not handing it over just yet." Amanda put her hand in her pocket to ensure the stone was still there. "Besides, I'm starting to get attached to it."

She looked at her watch. "It's almost time for Mom to pick us up. Let's quickly look through the Cretaceous Garden before she gets here."

"I don't blooming believe it!" Leah stomped after Amanda.

The Cretaceous Garden smelled earthy and damp with humidity. Some weird ferns and shrubs were scattered amongst the evergreens. One looked like a large question mark.

Amanda read from a sign that explained the garden was designed to give visitors a chance to experience a natural environment similar to what the dinosaurs lived in millions of years ago. The girls wound their way through the display of prehistoric looking plants until they came across a huge footprint.

"Oh my, this is an actual dinosaur footprint found right next to this museum."

"Are you sure it's real?" Leah pulled out her camera.

"It says so on the sign right here." Amanda pointed. "And this is a fossil tree stump. Imagine how old it is."

Someone in a cowboy hat rushed past the girls almost knocking Leah over.

"It was nice and peaceful in here until he showed up. How rude to push us aside like that. Are you OK, Leah?"

"Yes, I think so. I may have taken a picture though. I hung onto my camera because I didn't want to drop it. I think I accidently pushed the button."

"Let's see what you took?"

Leah and Amanda looked at the screen. The picture was on an angle and bit blurry. They both gasped when they saw the back of the intruder. Red hair stuck out below his cowboy hat.

"Do you think it was…"

"Maybe. But why was he rushing to get out of here?"

"I thought we'd seen the last of him," said Leah.

"It's time to meet Mom anyhow. There's an exit sign right over there."

Leah looked both ways when she got outside. "I sure don't want to meet up with Hank again."

"I don't think he even saw us. He was in too big of a rush to notice. I wonder who he was running from."

"Maybe he was afraid the T-Rex would get him." Leah laughed nervously. "There's your mom pulling up in front."

CHAPTER 15

D id you girls have a good time?" asked Amanda's mom.

"It was rad! I took heaps of photos to show my mates back home."

"We saw a bone that Aunt Mary found."

Mrs. Ross pulled out of the parking lot. "She was very excited when she discovered that bone. She's been involved in the museum since the beginning. By the way, I checked with her earlier and she is feeling much better. Would you like to stop at the gift shop before we head out to the Hoodoos?"

Leah looked up from her camera. "The what doos?"

"The Hoodoos," Amanda replied. "You'll love them. Just wait and see. More photo ops for you."

Once again they parked under the tail of the huge dinosaur at the Visitor Information Centre and gift shop. Inside the girls had fun choosing souvenirs. Amanda decided on a stuffed toy dinosaur. Leah bought a Triceratops golf club cover for her dad and a dinosaur head on a stick. By pulling on a string, the dinosaur's mouth opened, displaying its sharp teeth.

"My dinosaur can bite your dinosaur." Leah opened the mouth and placed it around the stuffy's leg.

"Ouch, that hurt. Stop biting me." Amanda pulled her dinosaur away.

"Please, don't break the toys until I've paid for them." Mrs. Ross took the items and waited in line at the till.

The girls looked through a rack of books and magazines at the back of the store.

"Do ya think you might learn something?" asked a familiar voice behind them.

Amanda's muscles tensed. She exhaled and turned around. "What...are...you...doing...here... Hank?"

"Looking for a stone that I know you have. I saw you show it to the guy at the museum." Hank smirked and held out his hand. "Give it to me and I'll leave you alone."

"It's just a stone. Why do you want it so bad?" asked Amanda.

"I need it and you don't, that's why. Gimme it!" Hank lunged toward Amanda.

Leah stepped forward and kicked him hard in the shin.

"Ow!" Hank doubled over, holding his leg.

Leah grabbed Amanda's hand. They ran through a nearby service door down a hallway and into a dark entrance where a group of children waited in line.

"OK, the next group can enter," announced a young woman wearing a T-shirt with *Drumheller Tourism* on it.

Amanda and Leah followed; looking back to be sure Hank hadn't followed them.

"We don't have tickets," whispered Leah.

"Shh. Maybe they'll think we're with this group."

"Your camp leader already gave me your tickets so go right into the dinosaur. There are 106 stairs to the viewing platform, so watch your step. Remember, only twelve people in the mouth at one time."

Amanda smiled at the young woman as they marched by.

While they ascended the giant T-Rex, they observed interesting mural paintings, fossil displays and an explanation of the construction. They read that The World's Largest Dinosaur is actually four and a half times the size of a real Tyrannosaurus Rex, weighs 145,000 pounds, stands 86 feet tall and is 151 feet long.

Amanda read from a story board. "It says here that this is actually a female T-Rex, and she is made almost entirely out of steel. I always think of dinosaurs as being male."

"Of course there were female dinosaurs, silly. How else would there be babies?"

They entered a spooky, dark area. "It feels like we have been swallowed by the T-Rex." Leah trembled as they walked past white skeleton bones painted on the inside walls.

Soon they emerged onto the viewing platform inside the gigantic mouth. Looking through the beast's enormous teeth, they could see the Red Deer River wind for miles through the magnificent badlands.

"This is quite amazing, Amanda." Leah brought out her camera and took pictures from every angle.

"There's Hank." Amanda pointed down to the parking lot. "Looks like he's lost something."

"Or someone." Leah laughed. "I bet he wonders where we disappeared to."

"Mom will be wondering too. We'd better get back down."

"Where did you go?" Mrs. Ross frowned when she saw the girls. "I paid for the items and you had disappeared. I thought you wanted to go inside the dinosaur?"

"That's OK, Mom. We don't feel like it anymore. We want to get to the Hoodoos. Right, Leah?" Amanda headed for the car.

Ω Ω Ω

A short drive through the badlands brought them to an area that looked like another planet with supernatural rock formations emerging from the ground.

Leah sucked in a quick breath as she stared at rocks

shaped like giant mushrooms. "Are those the Hoo-doos?"

"Pretty cool, eh?" replied Amanda. "You better hope your camera still has battery power."

Mrs. Ross's cell phone rang just as she parked the car beside a HandiBus. "I'm sorry, girls, but I have to take this call. It's important. Have a look around, but stay on the pathways. There are some good lookout spots to take pictures from."

The hot sun blazed in the clear blue sky as Amanda and Leah followed the walkway past cream coloured columns layered in various shades of brown, grey and rust. Flat stones, balanced precariously on top of the pillars, looked like they might fall off at any minute. Some stood alone while others were grouped together like a family of Hoodoos. No two were alike. At the top of a lookout, Leah held her camera in front of her and Amanda. She took a selfie of them in front of a huge Hoodoo framed by badlands.

"Why are they called Hoodoos?" asked Leah.

"We learned in school that the name 'Hoodoo' comes from the word 'voodoo' and was given to these forma-tions by the Europeans. We also learned that according to the Blackfoot and Cree traditions, the Hoodoos are believed to be petrified giants who come alive at night to hurl rocks at intruders."

"Well, they are kind of scary and I wouldn't want to

be here alone at night." Leah grimaced.

"Look, people are climbing the rocks behind the Hoodoos." Amanda pointed. "That looks like fun."

"Your mom said to stay on the walkways."

"I know the signs say we can't climb on the Hoodoos, but it doesn't say we can't climb on the badlands. It must be all right if other people are climbing over there. Let's check it out."

They left the walkway and Amanda led the way up the side of the badlands. She turned around and said, "Leah, hurry, it's a great view from up here. You can get some super pictures of all the Hoodoos."

"I'm coming." Leah was out of breath when she reached the top. "I should have brought my water with me. Blimey, it sure is hot."

She fumbled as she pulled out her camera from her pocket. It slipped out of her hand. The girls watched in horror as the camera tumbled down the rocky incline and behind a Hoodoo.

"Oh, no! My camera!" Leah scrambled after it.

Amanda followed her, slipping in her haste and scraping her hands as she tried to break the fall. She winced and brushed her hands on her jeans to get rid of the dirt and stones. When she finally caught up to Leah behind a large Hoodoo, she discovered her friend was not alone.

Hank stood grinning with the camera in his hand.

"Looking for this?"

Chapter 16

"Give...her...the...camera." Amanda glared at Hank.

"Sure thing, as soon as you give me the stone." Hank squinted. "I figure that's a fair trade."

"That's not your camera to trade with."

"Finders, keepers." Hank dangled the camera by the cord. "I could always drop it and step on it by accident."

Boots crunched on the rocks behind them.

"Are you threatening these two young women?"

Amanda turned around and detected a pair of dark blue trousers with a gold stripe down each side. She looked up and recognized the grey, short sleeved shirt, dark blue tie and policeman's hat of an RCMP officer.

Hank took a step backwards and muttered, "I found this here camera and...and was wondering if it belonged to one of them." His beet red face didn't help to make him sound very convincing.

"That's not what it sounded like." The officer held out his hand.

Hank gingerly placed the camera in the outstretched hand.

"Aren't you Hank McGavity? I heard you were gone from these parts."

Hank backed up further. "I was just about to leave, sir."

The RCMP officer glanced at the girls. "Was he bothering you?"

Amanda thought about the stone in her pocket, which may or may not be a precious artifact. Not wanting to get into any trouble with the police, she replied, "No. I think he was just teasing us."

Leah just stood there with her eyes wide open, staring at the young officer.

"You best be on your way then, Mr. McGavity. Keep your nose clean. I'll be keeping an eye on you."

Hank pulled his hat down low and turned around. Taking very large steps, he sprinted toward the parking lot.

The officer shook his head and turned to the girls. "I'm Constable Rob Turner of the Drumheller RCMP. Are you enjoying your visit to the Hoodoos?"

"Oh, yes," they said in unison.

"Is this your first time to see these crazy rocks?"

"I've been here before but it's the first time for my friend, Leah. She's visiting from England."

Leah grinned from ear to ear. "Are you really a...a Mountie? I thought you would look different though."

"I guess you expected the Red Serge and flat-brimmed Stetson. We only wear those for ceremonies, in parades and in the Musical Ride. Oh, and when we have our pictures taken for postcards." The young officer winked causing Leah to turn a scarlet red. "You be careful now. These badlands are not always safe. You should stay on the pathways. By the way, we're on the look out for some artifact thieves. If you see or hear anything out of the ordinary, let me know."

Amanda swallowed. She thought about the stone in her pocket and looked down at her feet. She hoped he couldn't read her mind.

"We'll let you know if we see anything suspicious."

The officer handed Amanda a business card, touched the rim of his hat and strode away.

Once he was out of earshot, Leah turned to Amanda. "Blimey, are they all that cute?"

"Oh, for heaven's sake. He's over twenty years old. Way too old for us."

"True, but he's very dreamy. I sure would love to see him in his dress uniform."

"He's just a Mountie. They're everywhere."

Leah smiled. "Well, you sure went gaga over the Bobbie in London, didn't you?"

Amanda's ears turned red. "Yeah, I guess so."

"Amanda! Leah! Over here." Someone waved at them from a group on a nearby lookout.

"It's Sharon and the kids from the hospital!" Amanda waved back.

Amanda and Leah found a path that led to the walkway and soon joined the other kids.

Sharon smiled and said, "This is fun isn't it? It's so great that the walkways and lookouts are wheelchair accessible, so we can all come up here to view the Hoodoos."

A nurse handed out drink boxes. She asked Amanda and Leah if they were thirsty.

"Thanks, I'm parched," said Leah as she accepted the apple juice.

"Be sure to put your empties in this recycle bin," said the nurse. "We don't want to litter this special place. We don't know how much longer it will be here."

Amanda reached for a juice box.

"Oh, my. What have you done to your hand? It's bleeding." The nurse examined her outstretched hand.

"I fell and scraped it on the rocks. It'll be OK."

"We had better clean it up for you." The nurse opened up a first aid kit and swabbed the cuts with disinfectant. Then she wrapped Amanda's hand with a gauze band-aid.

"You look like you've been in a fight with that plaster on your hand," said Leah.

"What's a plaster?" asked Sharon.

"I think that's what they call a band-aid in England," replied Amanda.

The nurse took some group shots of the patients including Amanda and Leah before the children had to leave.

"It was so great seeing you guys here," said Sharon before she climbed into the bus. "You should come to my brother's lacrosse game on Saturday, in Medicine Hat. It's a fundraiser for the hospital. If you've never seen a lacrosse game, Leah, you would really enjoy it."

"That sounds like fun. I'll ask my parents if we can go," said Amanda.

They waved as the bus pulled out of the parking lot revealing the Ross's SUV. Mrs. Ross rolled down the window. "Sorry, that call took longer than I thought it would. Did you enjoy the Hoodoos? Oh no! What did you do to your hand, Amanda? Honestly, I can't leave you alone for five minutes without you hurting yourself."

"It's nothing. I just fell on some stones and scraped it. A nurse cleaned it and wrapped it up like this. It looks worse than it is." Amanda held up her hand.

"There's blood on your jeans as well. We'd better get you home before anything else happens. Besides I have some more work to do in Calgary." She shook her head and started the car.

Once back home, Leah said to Amanda, "Your mom seemed annoyed. Maybe we shouldn't ask her to drive us places anymore."

"She gets like that sometimes. She works too hard and gets stressed. Mom needs to take a break once in awhile." Amanda placed the stone back on the bookshelf.

"And something else, why did you let Hank get off scot free? You should have told the Mountie that he was threatening us. That would've put an end to it."

"I know. It was just that I was scared Hank would tell him about the stone in my pocket and say I stole it or took it illegally from the badlands."

Leah sighed. "I do wish you would just get rid of it. It seems to be more trouble than it's worth."

Chapter 17

The next morning Don Ross entered the kitchen whistling. He spotted the girls eating cold cereal and asked, "How do you like those, who-do-you-think-you-are, Hoodoos?"

"They are totally brilliant," replied Leah.

"Oh, Dad, you think you're so funny, but you're so lame." Amanda punched her dad on the shoulder.

"Watch who you're calling lame." Amanda's dad pretended to punch her back.

"How did those rocks get like that, I wonder?" asked Leah.

"The Hoodoos were formed by the erosion from the water, wind and frost," said Amanda's dad while he poured himself a mug of coffee. "And you'll only find them in areas that have hot, dry summers and cold winters like here in southern Alberta."

"I see," said Leah as she took another mouthful of cereal.

"Or," added Mr. Ross. "The ancestors of the First Nations believed the Great Spirit turned evil giants into stone to stop them from bothering the people."

Leah shrugged. "That's an interesting story, but highly unlikely. Your first explanation makes more sense." Her face lit up. "By the way, we met a real Mountie when we were there."

Amanda kicked Leah under the table.

Leah gulped. "He was very nice and polite. He just wanted to know if we were enjoying the Hoodoos."

Amanda quickly changed the subject. "Why are you home, Dad, and in such a good mood?"

"It's the first day of our holidays, sweetie. I'm letting your mom sleep in. She had one of her headaches last night."

"So what are we doing today?"

"When Mom gets up, we'll drive down to Medicine Hat. The family reunion is tomorrow. We want to get settled into the hotel and have an early start to the pancake breakfast the next morning. Wait until you meet all of Amanda's crazy relatives, Leah."

"You mean there are more of them?"

"Oh yes, lots more," said Mr. Ross as he filled a bowl with cereal.

"Will Aunt Mary be there?" asked Amanda.

"Yes, she'll be coming with Uncle Jimmy and Aunt Marjorie and the kids."

Amanda smiled, happy about the chance to finally show Aunt Mary the stone.

That afternoon they loaded the car and headed down the Trans Canada Highway.

"This road is so straight," remarked Leah. "I can see forever."

The Ross family and their guest drove past flat, sage-green fields where delicate antelopes grazed. At times, little light-brown gophers scampered across the road, dodging traffic. Prickly tumbleweeds clung to barbed wire fences on either side of the highway. Occasionally, they drove past a herd of cows munching on grass and swishing their tails to keep the flies off their backs. The girls kept occupied by playing *I Spy* in the back seat.

Three hours later, after driving for what seemed like forever, they came over a hill and descended into a lush oasis. Spread out below them, a peaceful river flowed through the middle of a pretty city, surrounded by green trees and tidy brick houses.

A sign built of bricks read:

WELCOME TO MEDICINE HAT

"Finally, some trees and water," remarked Leah. She pointed in the distance. "And what's that?"

High on a hill, a huge red, white and blue structure overlooked the city.

"That's the World's Largest Tepee," said Amanda's dad. "It's in the Guinness Book of World Records."

"Can we stop and look at it up close, Dad?"

"I've driven by it so many times and have never stopped to look at it closely. Today is the day we are going to change that." Mr. Ross took the turnoff.

The tepee looked much larger when they got up close. Nothing covered the tall white poles that met at the top. A third way down, a red border with a zigzag design connected the poles. A blue border, with the same zigzag design, appeared two thirds of the way down. Under that were ten round storyboards facing inwards.

The girls walked inside the open tepee and looked up at the glaring sun.

"Wow, this is tall. How tall do you think this is?" asked Amanda.

"It says here that it is as tall as a twenty story building." Amanda's mom read from a brochure she picked up at the entrance. "The colours of the poles and designs mean something; white for purity, red for the rising and setting of the sun and blue for the flowing river."

The girls studied the hand-painted storyboards depicting native culture and history. Under each was a description. Leah read one that explained how Medicine Hat got its name.

"Sweet, so that explains it. It has to do with an eagle feather headdress with magical powers, found around here."

"There are a number of legends that tell the story of how this city got its name. They all have something to do with a Medicine Man's headdress, or hat," explained Mr. Ross.

All of a sudden Leah screamed. "S-something just ran across my feet. I think it ran down that hole." She pointed with a shaky finger.

"Nothing to worry about. It's just a gopher," said Amanda. "They're kind of cute. Look, there he is!"

A tiny, furry head popped up from a hole in the tall grass.

Leah relaxed. "He *is* awfully cute. It just startled me, that's all."

They were about to leave the area when Amanda spotted a sign on a notice board. "This is the lacrosse game Sharon told us about. It's later today. Can we go, Dad?"

"Sure, we have lots of free time. Let's check into the hotel first."

"I hope it's all right with you guys, but I think I'll just relax in the hot tub and maybe go to the spa," said Amanda's mom.

"That's a good idea, Evelyn. You stay at the hotel and relax; I'll take the girls to the game. It's been a long time since I've been to one. I used to play lacrosse in high school."

"I didn't know that, Dad."

Ω Ω Ω

Later, at the entrance to the arena, Amanda spotted Dan jump out of a van. He leaned inside and pulled out a long stick with a net shaped like a bicycle seat on the end. It looked like something to scoop small fish out of the water or pick apples off a tree.

"Hey, Dan," she called. "We've come to watch you play."

Dan grinned and walked over to them.

"Thanks for coming. Sharon said she saw you in Drumheller. This game is to raise money to send some of the sick children from the hospital to camp, you know." A sad look crossed Dan's face. "Some of those kids aren't going to get better."

Amanda didn't know what to say. She wanted to ask him what was wrong with Sharon but felt awkward. It didn't seem like the right time or place. She looked at her dad.

"Oh, Dan. You haven't met my dad. Dad, this is Dan."

Mr. Ross put out his hand. "Pleased to meet you, Dan. I played lacrosse when I was your age. I'm looking forward to the game."

Dan shook the outstretched hand. "What position did you play?"

"I played big stick, and you?"

"The same, defender."

"I look forward to seeing you play. Look girls, I'll go get the tickets and meet you back here."

"What is lacrosse anyway, is it like hockey?" asked Leah.

"Well sort of, it's really a combination of hockey, basketball and soccer. Our ancestors played it hundreds of years ago. They called it *baggataway*. The Europeans came and added a bunch of rules to make it more *civilized*." Dan chuckled.

"Why is it called lacrosse?" asked Amanda.

"When the French missionaries first saw the game, they thought the stick with the oval net on top looked like the staff carried by the Catholic bishops. The staff was called, '*la crosse*' in French. The name stuck. It's an exciting game with lots of fast action. Keep your eye on the ball. You'll enjoy it. By the way, Sharon said a guy with red hair ran out from behind a Hoodoo yesterday, just before you guys came around the same rock. Hank isn't still bothering you, is he?"

"Oh, it was nothing." Amanda looked away.

Dan put down his lacrosse stick. He placed both hands on her shoulders and looked into her eyes. "Amanda, promise me you will stay away from him. He's big trouble. I'm serious."

"Dan, hurry up!" called one of his teammates.

"Time to go and get suited up." Dan picked up his lacrosse stick. "Enjoy the game."

110

Chapter 18

The exciting game kept everyone's attention. With lightning speed, players ran up and down the field. A player cradled the bright orange ball in the webbing at the end of his stick until passing it on to a teammate. The opposing defenders tried everything possible to steal or knock the ball away with their sticks. The players ducked and wove their way toward the opposing goal, always wary of the other team's defenders. Many times Dan took the ball away from the opposition and passed it on to an attacker, who then shot the ball into the net for a score.

Amanda and Leah cheered the loudest when Dan's team won.

Men in cowboy hats arrived on the field to hand out prizes to the winning team and shake hands with all the players.

"Isn't that Mr. Rowlands?" Leah pointed to one of the men.

"It sure looks like him," replied Amanda.

After the prizes were handed out, Andy Rowlands

took the mike. "I hope you enjoyed this lacrosse game. Lacrosse is Canada's national summer sport, and is quickly becoming popular in other countries. I would like to thank you all for coming. The entire proceeds of this game will go to the Camps for Kids Project which enables seriously sick children to attend camp at no cost.

On behalf of the Alberta Cattleman's Association, I would like to make an additional donation of ten thousand dollars toward this project." The crowd cheered as Andy handed over a cheque to members of the hospital board. "Feel free to make an extra donation yourself, if you feel inclined," Andy added with a smile before handing over the mike.

As they drove to the hotel, Amanda said, "That was a lot of money Andy Rowlands donated."

"Many ranchers and farmers put money toward that donation," replied her dad. "Andy was just the spokesperson for the Cattleman's Association."

"Well, that was still very nice of them. Maybe your accounting firm could make a donation."

"Perhaps we will."

Ω Ω Ω

The next morning, they all drove out to a campground near a town called Seven Persons, for a pancake breakfast with about two hundred of Amanda's relatives.

Leah looked around. "You can't possibly be related to all of these people."

"You bet I am. Some are fourth or fifth cousins, but they are all related to my mom and me." Amanda waved to a group of younger children playing a game of marbles.

Uncle Jimmy grinned as he flipped pancakes. "And how many for our special visitor from England?" He plopped three big fluffy pancakes on Leah's paper plate before she could answer. "Hope you're hungry," he said as he put another three on Amanda's plate. Then he shouted, "We need more batter over here, boys. These hungry gals finished us off."

"Uncle Jimmy, you're embarrassing us. Is Aunt Mary here yet?"

"She'll be along shortly. She's coming with Marjorie and the kids. Enjoy the pancakes. There'll be an exciting scavenger hunt later." He winked at Leah and went back to making pancakes.

After breakfast, everyone joined in the three-legged races, a horseshoe tournament and baseball game. Then groups of young people were given a list and a pail for the scavenger hunt. Amanda and Leah teamed up with Gordon and Sarah.

Gordon looked at the list and said, "Let's take my truck. We can get everything way faster that way."

"Are you sure that's not cheating?" asked Amanda.

"It doesn't say we can't take a vehicle." Gordon opened the truck door. "Hop in and let's get this done."

Leah held the list. "The first thing on the list is a clothes peg. Now where are we going to find one of those?"

"Easy peasy. Just look for a clothes line." Amanda searched out the window. "There's one, behind that farm house."

Gordon made a sharp right hand turn and drove through an open gate with a sign over it that said, *Paradise Ranch*. He drove up to the house and honked the horn. No one seemed to be about. He jumped out of the truck, ran to the clothes line and removed one clothes peg.

"No one'll miss this." He dropped it in the pail and drove off.

"Next thing on the list is a red rock," read Leah.

"There's lots of red rocks at Red Rock Coulee," said Sarah. "It's not very far from here."

"Good idea. I'll drop you off at Red Rock Coulee. You can get the rock and other things on the list, like a wild flower and a feather, while I go into town and get a business card, a pet treat and a postcard." He studied the list. "If we split up it'll go faster. I've a feeling we're gonna win this scavenger hunt."

A few minutes later, Gordon dropped the girls off at the top of a hill covered with long grass that bent in the wind. The hill overlooked a shallow gorge dotted with huge reddish orange, round boulders.

"Are you sure he didn't drop us off somewhere on the moon?" asked Leah.

The girls surveyed the weird rocks that looked like meteorites.

"It's pretty desolate out here," said Sarah. "I'd hate to be here on my own."

A sign read:

CAUTION:
YOU ARE IN RATTLESNAKE COUNTRY

"I don't think I want to go down there if there are to be rattlesnakes," Leah said in a strained voice as she backed away.

"It'll be OK. You always hear them before you see them. I've been here before and I've never run into any," assured Amanda. "Just follow me."

The girls scrambled down to the rocks and soon found the perfect red rock for the game.

"Over here is a flower that would work." Leah bent down to pick a bright yellow flower growing between two rocks.

"That's called a buffalo bean," Sarah said. "It will be perfect."

The girls couldn't find a feather so they hiked deeper into the valley.

"Be careful you don't step on a cactus," Amanda cautioned Leah. "They are hard to see because they're the same colour as the grass."

"I thought cactus only grew in the desert," said Leah.

"What do you think this is? It's desert country, all right," said Sarah.

"What is that over there?" Leah pointed to a building on a knoll. A lone tree stood in front of it. Both the tree and the house had seen better days.

"Let's check it out." Amanda headed toward the weather worn building.

The door hung crooked like a broken leg and opened with a screech. A musty smell greeted them. A large wooden table, set for four, stood in the middle of the kitchen. A round loaf of bread rested on a thick plank, a rusty knife beside it. Amanda touched the bread. It was rock hard. Her eyes searched the shelves of preserves, bound together with cobwebs. She stepped closer and squinted to read the labels.

"Oh my gosh, these beet pickles are from 1938."

"Look at this," said Sarah.

A treadle sewing machine, like the ones seen in a museum, sat idle; the needle stuck in a lace trimmed hankie.

"It's as if the people living here left in the middle of the day," said Amanda. "I wonder what drove them away?"

"We should leave," said Leah. "This is starting to freak me out."

"Look at this old note nailed to the wall." Sarah read from a piece of yellowed paper:

> Seven miles to water
> Fifteen miles to wood
> You can have my desert homestead
> I'm leaving it for good

"Maybe that's why they left," said Leah as she edged toward the door.

A dusty photograph album on the piano bench caught Amanda's attention. She leafed through the discoloured pages. Elegant ladies in old fashioned dresses and fur coats smiled. Serious men in dark suits and black moustaches stared straight ahead. Happy babies all bundled up, snuggled in lacy prams, even though it looked sunny out.

Amanda turned another page. A sepia photograph of a dead person laid out in a coffin appeared. Chills ran up and down her spine. She quickly closed the album.

Bump!

"What was that noise?" Leah's eyes grew wide.

Bump!

"There it is again. I think it's in the attic. I'm out of here." Leah ran out the door.

Sarah followed close behind.

Amanda tripped over the piano stool.

"Wait for me," she called.

She picked herself up and ran for the door, catching the pocket of her shorts on a nail as she squeezed through. Once outside, she looked at the rip and thought, 'Darn, now Mom will be angry at me for wrecking my new shorts.'

She looked back, squinting at the glare coming from a small attic window. A face appeared in the window. Her stomach tightened. She looked again and no one was there.

CHAPTER 19

Gordon waited for them at the top of the hill. "Where were you guys? Did you get everything?" He frowned. "We need to get going if we want to win."

"We couldn't find a feather," said Sarah as they piled into the truck.

"Watch out the window while we drive down the road. There might be one," said Gordon.

They hadn't driven far when Amanda shouted, "There's one!"

The brakes screeched as Gordon stopped and then backed up.

Amanda jumped out and picked up the long black feather. She thought it might be from a crow. She looked up as another vehicle passed them going in the opposite direction, spraying rocks and dust.

"I wonder where they're going in such a hurry," said Amanda as she climbed back in the pick-up. "There's nothing up the road but Red Rock Coulee."

"Maybe they're looking for things for the scavenger hunt too," said Leah.

Gordon put the pick-up in gear. "That truck doesn't belong to anyone in our family."

After collecting the last few items on the list, they returned to the campground and proudly placed the bucket on the table where another cousin checked off each item.

"Well, it looks like you came in first. But, you used a vehicle and that's an unfair advantage. So you'll have to wait ten minutes. If no other team arrives with all the items, you'll be the winners."

Gordon's face fell. "Who made up that rule?"

"It's only fair," said Amanda. Sarah and Leah nodded in agreement.

"I guess so," mumbled Gordon.

Amanda spotted Aunt Mary chatting with a couple of older family members. "I'll be right back," she said leaving the others to await the outcome.

"Aunt Mary, how are you?" Amanda bent down to give the older woman a hug.

"I'm much better thank you. I hear you have been busy with your friend from England."

"Yes, we have been having loads of fun. We saw a bone at the dinosaur museum that you dug up."

"Oh, that was a long time ago. You were going to show me that piece of rock you found. The one with an interesting mark on it."

Amanda put her hand in her pocket and felt around.

Her heart stopped. She slowly shook her head and whispered, "No." The stone wasn't there.

"Is something the matter, Amanda?" asked Aunt Mary.

"I-I'll be back. I have to go." Amanda turned around. With her eyes glued to the ground, she weaved her way to the others.

Leah's face lit up when she saw Amanda. "No one else has shown up. It looks like we won!"

"Um, oh, that's nice." Amanda kept looking at the ground, hoping she would see the missing stone.

"You don't seem very excited about us winning. What's the matter? What are you looking for?"

"The stone, it's not in my pocket anymore. I remember putting it there just before we left this morning to show Aunt Mary, and now it's gone." Amanda bit her bottom lip to stop from crying. "Maybe it fell out at the old house in Red Rock Coulee."

"Well, I'm glad it's gone. Now you can enjoy yourself and not think about it anymore. Let's collect our prizes." Leah skipped away with Sarah.

Amanda collapsed on a nearby bench. 'Where could it have gone?' She pondered and reached in her pocket again just to be sure. She felt the rip. 'It must have fallen out when I ripped my pocket at the old house. I need to go back and find it. But how can I get there?'

Leah brought Amanda an ice cream Dixie cup.

"Cheer up. Gordon said there's going to be a Little Britches Rodeo for the little kids. That ought to be fun to watch."

Amanda removed the wrapping from the small wooden spoon that came with the Dixie cup and dipped it in. The cool ice cream felt good as it slid down her dry throat.

"Thanks, Leah. Let's go watch the mutton busting."

"The...what?"

"You'll see."

Amanda and Leah followed a crowd of family members to a small corral set up in a field. They watched as adults held onto a nervous sheep to keep it still, while a little child, around five or six years old, was placed on top of it. The adult let go of the sheep. The child held onto the sides of the woolly animal for dear life and rode down the field until he tumbled off. All the little kids got a chance to ride a sheep. The young buckaroo who stayed on the longest, won a prize.

"They are sooooo cute," said Leah. "I have never seen anything quite so adorable."

Someone dressed as a rodeo clown helped the kids up and delivered them to their parents. No one got hurt. The kids wore helmets and were so little the sheep barely felt them on their backs.

"This is more my kind of rodeo," said Amanda. "I wonder who the rodeo clown is."

"They hired some guy," said Gordon who had just come up behind them. "I offered to do it but they wanted someone with rodeo experience to make sure everyone was kept safe. Hey, barbeque is on. Hope you guys are hungry."

Amanda kept thinking about how she could get back to Red Rock Coulee. She was sure the rock had to be there. She really wanted to show it to Aunt Mary and find out why everyone was so interested in it. Just as she opened her mouth to bite into her hamburger, she saw the rodeo clown get into Gordon's truck.

She looked over to where Leah and Sarah chatted with some other cousins. Amanda put down her paper plate and ran over to the truck just as the clown started to back up and turn around. Realizing she couldn't stop him, she grabbed the tailgate and swung onto the back as he drove out of the campground. She hid behind a bale of hay.

It wasn't long until the truck stopped. Amanda peeked around the bale. They were on the hill overlooking Red Rock Coulee.

'Well, at least I made it here,' she thought.

The driver got out of the cab. He took off his clown wig and hat revealing a head of red hair. He loped down the valley through the huge red boulders.

'Hank was the rodeo clown? Why did he steal Gordon's truck? And what is he doing here?' Amanda's mind raced.

She waited a few minutes. When Hank was no longer in sight, she climbed out of the back of the truck, brushing the hay off her clothes. In the dusk, the red rocks cast eerie shadows as she made her way down into the coulee. Amanda wondered if she would be able to find the house again. A rattling sound in the grass stopped her in her tracks.

"I'm sorry I disturbed you, rattlesnake, wherever you are. Please let me pass without striking me." Amanda's voice trembled.

With her eyes glued to the ground in front of her, she placed one foot in front of the other as if she were walking on broken glass. She rounded a corner and saw the lone bent and gnarled old tree. The dull grey, weather-beaten house behind it almost blended into the landscape. It appeared much more daunting than in the bright daylight. A shiver ran through Amanda. She wished she hadn't come by herself. 'What was I thinking? Perhaps Leah was right; it was after all, only a stone. And where had Hank gone?'

Amanda shrugged. 'Since I'm here, I'd better look for the stone.'

Searching the ground leading up to the door, she found nothing. The crooked door screeched as she pushed it open and entered the house. Things looked the same as earlier in the day, but a faint smell of stale cigarette smoke mixed with the musty scent. Kneeling down in the dim light, she felt around the floor.

"It's got to be here," she whispered under her breath.

A noise came from upstairs. The hair on her arms lifted. She heard it again. This time it sounded like footsteps coming down a ladder.

Amanda slowly stood up. She turned to the half open door. Her legs refused to move. An arm reached around her and held her tight. She felt hot breath on her neck.

"Are you looking fer something?"

CHAPTER 20

L et go of me, Hank!" Amanda squirmed and kicked. More angry than scared, she said, "You are the worst...person...ever. What are you doing here, anyway?"

"I heard you tell your friend you dropped the rock here when you were snooping around earlier today. I've come to find it, and you're not going to stop me." Hank dragged Amanda to a ladder.

"I'm not going up there."

"Oh yes, you are. You can scream all you want, no one will hear you. There ain't a soul for miles."

Hank pushed Amanda up the ladder into the dark attic and bound her wrists and feet with a rope.

"I know I don't need to do this, but just in case." He tied a handkerchief around her mouth. Picking up a flashlight, he went back downstairs.

Amanda looked around the gloomy attic. Through the dust and cobwebs, she made out a crumpled up sleeping bag in one corner. A package of cigarettes and a clown suit lay beside it. Squinting, she detected what looked like crosses in another corner. She could hear Hank moving things around downstairs.

'I hope he doesn't find that stone.' Amanda's mind raced. 'How can I get out of here before everyone wonders where I've got to? How stupid of me to jump onto the back of the truck like that.'

The front door screeched open and an angry voice said, "Hank McGavity, what in blazes are you doing here?"

"This is my family's property. I have every right to be here. What're you doing here?"

"We're looking for someone."

The voice sounded familiar to Amanda, but it wasn't any of her family. She wondered who else would be looking for her.

She dragged herself over to the crosses. With her legs bound together, it was slow going. As she got closer, Amanda could see the crosses had names engraved on them. They looked like old grave markers. She shuddered.

"Dan and Ed Crow Feather, get out of my house. Right now!" Amanda heard Hank yell.

"This isn't your house, Hank. The government took it over years ago when your grandfather couldn't pay the mortgage. It's now part of the Provincial Park Natural Area. You know that."

Amanda recognized Dan's voice. 'How did he know

where to find me?'

'I need to get his attention.' She tried nudging the crosses with her feet but they wouldn't move.

"What in tarnation is that cowboy doing here?" Hank hollered.

A dog barked as the door squeaked open.

"Andy Rowlands?" exclaimed Dan.

Amanda kicked at the crosses with her feet. They fell over and crashed onto the floor of the attic.

"What's that noise? Is someone up there?" asked Dan.

"It's nothing, probably just rats," said Hank.

"I think I better have a look."

"You do that, Dan, while I ask this young man a few questions. Don't worry, Ed, I won't let Hank hit you again." There was no mistaking Andy's voice.

Amanda's face lit up when Dan appeared at the top of the ladder. He rushed over to her.

"Are you OK?" Dan asked as he removed the handkerchief and quickly untied her hands and feet.

"Better now that you showed up. How did you know I was here anyway?"

"I didn't. Let's get you downstairs."

Andy Rowlands looked surprised. "Amanda, what are you doing here? I thought you were at a family reunion."

"I came looking for something."

"It wouldn't happen to be a stone; a special stone with writing on it?" asked Andy.

Bart ran over to Amanda and looked up at her, his tail wagging. Amanda patted his head.

"What is so special about that stone anyway?" asked Amanda.

"I believe it is part of a set of stones that make up a large petroglyph of a buffalo hunt," Andy explained. "Over the years the mural has crumpled, scattering many pieces around the area. If they are collected, the mural could be reassembled. The museum is very interested in obtaining these stones. The mural is of great significance to the history of our province."

Amanda gulped. Bart wandered over to the piano, sniffed a leg and sat under the bench. Just before he settled down, Amanda thought she saw the stone under the piano. She looked away.

"Why does everyone want the stone?"

Ed said, "This stone belongs to our people. It is part of our history and should stay with The Blackfoot Confederacy. We already have some of the stones. That one must have fallen out of my pocket at the Stampede parade."

"Yes, it did. I picked it up and called after you, but you didn't hear me."

"The stones belong to the museum. I have some as well. We should give all of them to the museum so the experts there can reassemble the mural," said Andy.

"Well it's gone now. Amanda lost it so you can all leave." Hank glared at Amanda.

"Ya, well why were you holding Amanda captive in the attic, you scum bag?" asked Dan. "You just want the stone to sell to the highest bidder, don't you? I've heard about your gambling debts." He grabbed Hank by the shirt collar.

Andy stepped between them. "Now, boys, there's been enough fighting."

Dan let go of Hank. "If the museum would pay for the stones, we could use the money to send Sharon to a hospital in New York City. They could help her get better. We need that last stone to make up one part of the mural. Come on Amanda; let's get you back to your family."

Amanda swallowed and whispered, "I think I know where it is."

Everyone looked at her and said, "You do? Where?"

No one noticed Hank pick up a poker by the potbelly stove. He pointed it at Amanda. "No one is going anywhere until she tells me where it is."

Dan moved toward Amanda.

"If you move another step, I'll hurt her with this." Hank pushed the poker in front of Amanda's face.

Amanda felt faint. She squeezed her eyes shut. Her chin trembled.

"Put that down right now, Hank McGavity!"

An RCMP officer in full dress uniform appeared at the door and pushed his way in front of Andy, Ed and Dan.

Hank dropped the poker and looked around for an escape.

Constable Turner grabbed Hank and handcuffed him to the potbelly stove.

"It's safe to come in now," the officer said.

The old door swung open. A frightened Leah ran in. "Amanda?" She looked around and then rushed towards her. "Amanda!" Leah put her arms around her before she fell to the floor. "Are you all right?"

Amanda opened her eyes to see Aunt Mary bending over her and burst into tears. "Oh, Aunt Mary, I'm sorry. I'm so sorry. I caused all this trouble. The stone is...is over there." She pointed to Bart with a trembling finger.

"Under the dog?" asked Leah.

"No, under the piano. Right by the leg."

Constable Turner walked over to the piano and bent down. Reaching around the dog, he retrieved the stone and held it between his thumb and finger.

"Is this what everyone is looking for?"

CHAPTER 21

Many hugs greeted Amanda when she returned to the reunion. Her parents were so relieved they kept hugging and kissing her.

"How did you know where to find me and why did Constable Turner show up when he did?" Amanda had lots of questions.

"Well, when Gordon found his truck gone, he had a fit. Not long after, we realized you were missing as well," Leah explained. "I remembered you were upset about losing that stone, so I mentioned to Aunt Mary that maybe you had gone back to the old house at Red Rock Coulee. At first we thought maybe you took Gordon's truck. But then I decided, not even you would be that daft to take a truck when you can't even drive."

Amanda's dad jumped in the conversation. "I called the RCMP immediately and within minutes Constable Turner showed up. He had been part of a Musical Ride demonstration in Bow Island and heard the call on his radio as he was heading home. Leah and Aunt Mary insisted on going along to show him where to find the place. Mom and I stayed here in case you showed up. We've never been so worried."

With his arm around Amanda's shoulder, Mr. Ross turned to the constable. "We can't thank you enough for returning our daughter safely." He shook the police officer's hand warmly. "Now what is this about a rare artifact?"

Amanda and Leah explained everything.

"I'm so sorry I kept it. I just wanted to show it to Aunt Mary. I didn't think it was valuable at first. What will happen to it now?"

"The museum will decide what to do with it. It's in good hands," said Aunt Mary as she patted Amanda on the head. "All that matters is that you are safe, my dear."

Ω Ω Ω

Back in Calgary, a few days later, Amanda helped Leah pack. "I wish you could stay longer. It was so much fun having you here. It was like having a sister to do stuff with."

"Look, Amanda, you may not have a sister, but you have a huge family that loves you tons. You should have seen how worried everyone was when they thought you had been abducted."

"They thought I had been abducted?"

"Well, yes. When the truck and you disappeared,

they thought someone had taken you. Then when Uncle Jimmy asked if anyone had seen Hank McGavity, I couldn't believe it. I asked him why he wanted Hank. Uncle Jimmy told us he wanted to pay him. He'd heard Hank was in need of some cash, so he hired him to be the rodeo clown. That's when I put two and two together. I suggested we go to the old house at Red Rock Coulee. Just then Constable Turner showed up, in his dress uniform. OMG did he look fabulous!"

"Can we focus on my rescue instead of how good the officer looked?"

"Oh, yes. Aunt Mary and I jumped in his police cruiser and explained things as he sped out to the site. He sure caught Hank off guard, didn't he?"

Amanda shivered as she recalled how frightened she was with the poker inches from her face.

"You're right. I am lucky to have a family that cares about me. I know my parents work a lot but they do love me." With tears in her eyes, she smiled at Leah. "I'm also lucky to have such a good friend like you. You saved my life. Thanks." She gave Leah a great big hug.

"I wasn't such a good friend though, was I?" Leah shook her head. "I should have convinced you to turn in the stone right away. And I shouldn't have let you out of my sight at the reunion."

"I should have listened to you in the first place. And I guess it was kind of stupid of me to jump on the back of the truck."

Leah thought for a minute and then laughed, "That must have been funny to see."

They were both laughing when Mrs. Ross entered the room.

"Guess what? I just got off the phone with Aunt Mary. You are both invited to a meeting downtown with the Royal Tyrrell Museum Board of Directors tomorrow morning. We'll have to take you straight to the airport from there, so you best get all packed, Leah."

Ω Ω Ω

The next morning Amanda, her parents, Leah, Aunt Mary, Andy Rowlands, Constable Turner, Dan, Ed and Sharon Crow Feather sat at a boardroom table with some people from the Royal Tyrrell Museum. It all seemed very stuffy and official to Amanda. She worried they might reprimand her for keeping the stone.

The man they saw talking to Andy at the museum got up and cleared his throat. "We are pleased that we now have enough pieces of the petroglyph to re-create the mural of a buffalo hunt, as it was thousands of years ago.

We have many people to thank for this. First of all we'd like to thank Andy Rowlands from the Bar U Ranch for his generous donation of stones from his family collection. We would also like to acknowledge, with gratitude, the donation of stones from the Crow Feather family and members of the Siksika Nation. We understand the importance of these stones to you and the First Nations people. The mural will be dedicated to your ancestors."

The man took a sip of water and turned to Amanda and her family. Amanda held her breath.

"We would also like to thank Mary Johnson for her tireless support of the museum. A big thank you also goes to her great-niece, Amanda Ross, who helped return a stone we had been looking for." He pulled the stone from a plastic bag and held it up. "This stone has the mark of a buffalo hoof drawn on a rock face many years ago. It fits in with the others to complete the mural."

Everyone clapped and Amanda beamed. Aunt Mary squeezed her arm.

"As much as we appreciate these stones, the museum is unable to pay for them. But, we can make a donation." He turned to Sharon.

"We are prepared to give you a cheque to cover your trip to New York City and all medical expenses. We wish you a speedy recovery."

Dan gave his little sister a hug. Amanda thought she saw a tear in his eye.

Everyone met outside after the meeting and shook hands. Amanda and Leah took turns hugging Sharon.

"We hope you get better soon," said Amanda.

"Oh, I know I will. The doctors in New York will fix me up. Let's keep in touch by email."

"We will," said Amanda and Leah together.

"You were very brave, Amanda. I'm glad you didn't hand the stone over to Hank." Dan patted her on the shoulder. "Everything worked out fine in the end."

Smiling, Constable Turner approached the girls. "I understand you're going back home today, Leah."

Leah just nodded her head and swallowed as her face turned a deep pink.

"I brought you a souvenir to take back with you." He handed her a postcard with a picture of an RCMP officer in dress uniform. "Safe travels."

After he left, the girls looked at the postcard. The RCMP officer on the front was Constable Rob Turner himself. They turned the card over and saw he had signed it to Leah.

"I will treasure this forever." Leah carefully put the postcard in her backpack.

On the way to the airport Leah said, "Thanks for a brilliant holiday, Amanda." She frowned. "But when will we see each other again?"

"I'm sure something will come up." Amanda grinned. "It always does."

Acknowledgements

I would like to thank everyone involved in making this book come to be. My critique partners, Cyndy Greeno, Marion Iberg, Yvonne Pont and Sheila MacArthur who provided encouragement, honest feedback, brutal editing and some good laughs. I will be forever indebted to all of you. To my talented and wise publisher, Michelle Halket of Central Avenue Publishing who designs the perfect covers for my books and provides the motivation to continue; thanks for believing in me and my Amanda stories.

Thanks to the good folks at the Bar U Ranch who spent time with me; sharing stories and providing a perfect setting for part of the book. A great big thank you goes to my grandson Jesse who was my research assistant during our travels around southern Alberta. He pointed out things I would have missed.

I would like to thank Hope Johnson (1916 – 2010), who fuelled my interest in palaeontology and the rich history of Alberta many years ago. I based my character of Great Aunt Mary loosely on this remarkable woman I was honoured to have known.

I want to acknowledge my parents and my great big wonderful Alberta family, for providing me with an amazing childhood full of love and fond memories. I thank all of you from the bottom of my heart.